Dear Reader

I live with an ever-chan... wonderful men and wom... the world around us. As ... they mirror our own struggle to find our true soulmates. As their hearts are touched our hearts are touched. As they face life's ordeals we face them. I love creating strong, tender men and spirited, determined women who fight to reach the ultimate happy ending we all long to attain in our own lives.

When I create my stories I try and tap into the universal emotions we all share. I hope you'll enjoy the story of Piper and Gideon, two individuals who loved each other, lost that love and now struggle to find it again. To me that rediscovery of a love that transcends all hardship resonates with a depth of passion that is the core of true romance. It keeps me returning to Tender Romances™ as an avid reader because it's a journey I love to take again and again. And I hope it's a journey you'll continue to take with me.

Love

Day Leclaire

Day Leclaire is the multi-award-winning author of more than thirty novels. Her lively, warmly emotional style has won tremendous worldwide popularity and many publishing honours, including: the Colorado Award of Excellence and Golden Quill awards, two years running; five nominations for the prestigious Romance Writers of America RITA award; plus several awards from *Romantic Times Magazine*, including their Career Achievement Award.

Day's romances sweep readers into a compelling, uplifting world of romance, where tough yet tender men are tamed by spirited, likeable women. Her stories sparkle with humour and a depth of emotion that really touches the heart. She makes you care about her characters as much as she does. In Day's own words, 'I adore writing romances and can't think of a better way to spend each day.'

Look out for THE WHIRLWIND WEDDING,
continuing Day's *Wedded Blitz* trilogy,
coming soon!

Recent titles by the same author:

THE PROVOCATIVE PROPOSAL*
THE MARRIAGE PROJECT

*Wedded Blitz trilogy

THE
BRIDE PRICE

BY

DAY LECLAIRE

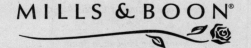

MILLS & BOON®

To friends who are there when the crunch times
are at their crunchiest. To Felicia Mason and Carolyn Greene
with my love, thanks, and deepest appreciation.

*First published in Great Britain 2002
Harlequin Mills & Boon Limited,
Eton House, 18-24 Paradise Road, Richmond, Surrey TW9 1SR*

© Day Totton Smith 2001

ISBN 0 263 82998 7

Set in Times Roman 10½ on 12¼ pt.
02-0402-49683

*Printed and bound in Spain
by Litografia Rosés, S.A., Barcelona*

PROLOGUE

Old Mill Run, Colorado

THEY ringed him like jackals surrounding a predator they were too apprehensive to take on by themselves.

Gideon ignored them, his attention focused on the more immediate danger—the man determined to beat him into the ground. Close by, the charred ruins of a hundred-year-old flour mill smoldered, the fire that had swept through it gutting a full year of painstaking renovation. Wisps of smoke invaded the circle, briefly obscuring his view, and he blinked against the sting, shaking back his sweat-dampened hair.

"I didn't burn your mill," he gritted out.

"Bull." Spencer's voice came in short, swift pants. "You were seen!"

"You're a liar!"

"Who else would have reason to do it?"

"How about you? I'll bet the insurance money will come in handy now that your old man is gone." Gideon's taunt was met by such a powerful fist to the chin that it sent him reeling.

"There is no insurance money, you bastard!" Spencer shouted. "All I had was tied up in that mill."

"I didn't burn it." Gideon stayed down, trying one final time to end the fight peacefully. It was a futile gesture, but one he felt obligated to attempt. "If you don't believe me, ask your sister."

5

"Leave Piper out of this. Your relationship with her is over."

Something primitive sparked to life, an elemental drive to protect and hold what belonged to him. "She's mine," he warned in a guttural voice. "She'll always be mine. No one is going to take her from me. Not even you."

"No?" Challenge was met with challenge. "You've ruined me and I swear I'm going to make you pay. You're garbage, Hart. You always have been. Always will be."

It was the final straw. Gideon had spent too many years fighting to protect his name and reputation. He'd be damned if he'd let Spencer destroy it now. Not over something he didn't do. Picking himself off the ground, he wiped the blood from the corner of his mouth. And then he attacked.

The next several minutes were vicious, neither man giving ground. The crowd surrounding them called encouragement to Spencer, quick to side with the town's golden boy. Gideon made the mistake of moving too close to the edge of the circle and was rewarded with a staggering slam to the back. Boots shot out of nowhere, pitching him off balance. But he'd been in his fair share of barnyard brawls, all with the odds against him, and he'd managed to come out on top. If he wanted to win this one, he'd have to find a way to even the current odds.

Finally he managed to knock Spencer through the circle, scattering the crowd. It was the opening he needed to finish the fight. He balled his hand, prepared to put his opponent down when a brutal kick swept his feet out from under him. Gideon went down hard, momentarily stunned. He suspected he'd cracked at least one of his ribs. It hurt to breathe, hurt to move. Not that he had any choice. In another second Spencer would be on him. Rolling, he forced himself to his feet.

They were close to the river now, near a ten-foot drop-off. It was either him or Spence, and he was damned if it was going to be him. Gathering every last ounce of energy, he drew back his arm.

Someone grabbed him from behind and he roared in frustration, shaking them off with an ease that had to come from an excess of adrenaline. Or perhaps it came from pure testosterone. All he knew was that something within him was raging out of control. Free once again, he launched himself at Spencer, ending the battle with a single, powerful right hook. Spence went down without a sound, hitting the ground with painful force.

And then the surrounding jackals went mad and Gideon disappeared beneath the ravenous pack.

CHAPTER ONE

Denver, Colorado
Five years later...

THE board meeting wasn't going the way he'd planned.

Gideon Hart folded his arms across his chest and regarded the chaos breaking loose around him. The owners and representatives of the three companies he'd recently purchased had already come to blows. Two nursed black eyes, another a swollen jaw and a fourth a chipped tooth. One was so drunk, she could be poured down the elevator shaft and into her limo. And the caterer he'd hired to provide them with lunch had decided to join the drunken mêlée by gulping from a bottle of his best Lafite Rothschild, after which she'd managed to set the dessert table on fire while attempting to ignite the crêpes Suzette.

But the pièce de résistance had to be the arrival of Piper Montgomery.

He hadn't expected her to crash the party. Hell, he hadn't expected to see her ever again. But she erupted from the elevator with all the determination of an avenging angel, dressed in a yellow so brilliant, it looked like a flaming sun had exploded to life in their midst. How long had it been since they were last together? Four years? Five? His mouth twisted. Five years, two months and twelve days. But who was counting?

She paused inside the doorway and lifted the Leica

camera strung around her neck, snapping off a quick series of shots. Nothing had changed, it would seem. Photography was still a vital part of her life, her take on the world around her expressed through a Carl Zeiss lens. Lowering the camera, her gaze swept the room, no doubt searching for him. Damn, but she looked good. Her hair was shorter than before, just clipping her shoulder blades, though still ruler-edge straight and still streaked with shades of blond ranging from sun-bleached white to a light sandy brown. She also had a figure capable of bringing men to their knees and blue eyes so direct and passionate they made most people uncomfortable. But he wasn't most people.

He waited patiently for her to zero in on him. A moment later her focus reached the corner where he stood and for an instant neither of them moved, an eternity passing in that split second. A darkness settled in her eyes, like night eclipsing day. Was she remembering their parting? Or was their current situation responsible for igniting the pain he read there?

Her jaw tightened, and with a defiance he couldn't mistake, she popped off another series of photos—this time aimed in his direction. Finished, she started toward him, her sunstruck yellow dress swirling around her knees with each determined stride. Not even the hysteria exploding around her slowed her approach. Skirting one battleground, she thrust straight through another, an elbow to the gut sending a beefy combatant reeling, while a well-placed stab from a deadly pair of high heels put a swift end to any thought of retaliation from his partner.

Gideon left his stance, clearing a path between them with ruthless determination. It wasn't concern for her safety that drove him to meet her halfway, he tried to tell himself. Hell, no. He didn't give a damn what happened to her. His mouth twisted. *Liar.* He made a living bursting other people's delusionary bubbles and here he was creating one of his own. He cared what happened, all right. He cared because he planned to destroy Piper's brother. Unfortunately that meant if Piper got in the way, he'd be forced to either move her out of his path, or take her down, as well.

"Hello, pipsqueak."

She bristled at the nickname. "You son of a—"

He didn't give her an opportunity to finish her greeting. Hell, it didn't take much imagination to figure how it would have ended. Sweeping her camera aside, he thrust his hand into her hair and tipped her into his arms. Then he sealed her mouth with his. She fell into him, her body colliding with delicious force.

She tasted even better than he remembered, hot and sweet and buttery soft, every bit of her edged with a potent vibrancy he'd never found in another woman. Her lips were wide and firm, melding with his as though they'd been specifically shaped with him in mind. Or perhaps his had been shaped just for her. She fit in his arms with a perfection he'd almost forgotten, joining instinctively at thigh, hip and chest.

Her figure had altered somewhat over the years, her legs and belly and arms leaner than the twenty-year-old he'd last held, her breasts and buttocks more lush than he recalled. But that was the only notable difference. All the qualities that mattered, that had attracted him to her in the first place, remained the same. It was there in the tender strength of her touch and the uncompromising determination of her gaze. She even tasted of resilient feminine energy.

He inhaled deeply, drawing her spicy scent into his lungs, absorbing her essence into his pores. Heaven help him, he could drown in her, lose all pretense at common sense and rationality. He traced his hand down her spine, locking them closer together. She didn't fight as he'd expected. Nor did she melt into the embrace as he'd hoped. Instead she ran the heel of her pumps along his calf. It served as an effective warning. He'd already seen the damage she could inflict with that particular feminine weapon.

"Okay, okay. You win this time," he murmured against her mouth.

"Correction. I win every time."

"Every time?" Snatching a final kiss, he fought the primitive urge that demanded he toss her over his shoulder and carry her off to a place where they could bring their renewed acquaintance to a more earthy conclusion. Instead he released her and fought to conceal his craving behind a civilized mask. It wasn't easy. Donning the mask of civilization never had been. Not for him. "Fair warning, sweetheart. That's about to change."

She took a hasty step backward and visibly fought for control. It would seem he wasn't the only one affected. His kiss had more of an impact than she cared to admit. "Dammit, Gideon. What did you do that for?"

"What? Kiss you?" He shrugged. Wasn't it obvious? "I wanted to."

"And whatever the great G.W. Hart wants, he gets. Is that it?"

"Words to live by."

"Words more likely to crash and burn by." She glanced around the room, her gaze falling on the smoldering remains of the dessert table, and she snapped off another picture, her actions both instinctive and practiced. Lifting an eyebrow, she returned her attention to him. "Problem with the caterer?"

He released a sigh. "A small case of pyromania. Negligible, really. Nothing to worry about."

Her mouth twitched and she finally broke down and laughed. The sound stirred something deep in his soul, something beyond his reach—something he'd thought himself incapable of feeling again. "Honestly, Gideon. Why am I not surprised to find you hosting a party where full-fledged warfare has broken out?"

"It's a knack." He gently shifted her to one side as a decanter of extremely expensive scotch soared by, splintering against the far wall. "Would you like some pointers?"

"I'll pass, thanks."

Time to get down to business. "Now, where were we?"

"I was about to call you a son of a—"

"And I took care of that with a kiss." He was pleased to see that his grim warning didn't escape her notice. "I assume you're here on Spencer's behalf?"

"We need to talk." The shouting escalated and she raised her voice to be heard over the din. "Somewhere private, if you don't mind."

He jerked his head toward the door leading from the conference room. "My office."

This time as they traversed the room, Gideon placed himself between Piper and harm's way. The fighting had slowed, the combatants tiring. Even the couple of swings aimed in his direction were halfhearted at best. That didn't stop Piper from attempting to jump into the fray, no doubt in the hope of ending the conflict. Though she'd never been one to back away from trouble, she'd always tried to find peaceful solutions to even the most disastrous situations. It had been key to her nature when he'd known her and he doubted anything had changed in recent years.

He stopped her from trying to deal with the current battle the simplest and most effective way available to a man of his nature. He clamped an arm around her waist and locked her to his side. It also prevented her from utilizing her camera. "You have to be the only woman I've ever met foolish enough to wade into a fistfight and risk your own well-being out of concern for the brawlers."

"Someone will get hurt if you don't stop them, Gideon."

He shrugged. "That's their choice. If they want to fight through their problems, let them. But I suggest you stay out of it. Fighting other people's battles is guaranteed to get you hurt. I'd have thought you'd learned your lesson the last time you made that mistake."

Pain exploded in her gaze, catching him totally off guard. "Not nice, Gideon. Before you were only ruthless. But I see you've become cruel."

What the *hell* was she talking about? "Explain that—"

Spinning, she evaded his grasp. "Ladies and gentlemen!" she called out. "Listen to me, please. You'll be delighted to know that Mr. Hart has changed his mind. There's no further need for argument."

For a split second there was absolute silence. Then everyone cheered. One poor man sank to the floor and blubbered like a baby. Piper took a single look at him and turned a gaze so filled with outrage on Gideon that if he'd been any other man he'd have flinched. Did she realize the power of those eyes? She must. Women always took advantage of whatever natural assets they possessed.

The camera went into action again. Not that it slowed the accusations she hurled his way. "You made him cry. You truly are a son of a bitch, Gideon. That's how I'm going to label these shots. 'SOB in action.'"

"No," he corrected. "*You* made him cry. And he'll be crying even harder when he finds out you lied to him."

"You're going to fix this," she informed him in a fierce undertone. "You're going to fix this before anyone else is hurt."

"Like I'm going to fix things with Spencer?"

"Yes."

He shouldn't touch her. Giving in to the impulse offered no advantage whatsoever. Even so, he couldn't resist tucking a silken lock of her hair behind one ear. "You always were a dreamer. It was a quality I liked about you, once upon a time."

Her chin shot up at that. "I was never a dreamer. In fact, I was the most realistic of any of us. But I do expect the best from people."

"You photograph the best within people," he corrected.

"And I still do, maybe because I always hope that basic goodness will eventually win out over people's more negative qualities."

"How do you handle the disappointment?"

The whir of the camera paused. "Spoken like a true cynic." She slanted him a speculative glance. "It'll be interesting to develop my film. I wonder if I'll find any goodness left in you.''

''Doubtful. But you already knew that, didn't you?'' The man on the floor had stopped sobbing. Climbing to his feet, he made a beeline toward them. ''Time to go,'' Gideon announced.

Dropping his arm around Piper's shoulders, he opened the door and left disaster behind. From the chaos of the boardroom, they stepped into a dimly lit corridor filled with an intense silence. It provided a disconcerting counterpoint to the noise and confusion they'd escaped.

''Good grief, Gideon.''

Piper stopped in her tracks in order to absorb her surroundings. The hallway gave the impression of stretching into infinity, an illusion he'd paid an impressive amount of money to achieve. It was as though some unseen entity drew all the light and energy from the surrounding area, leaving behind an unsettling stillness. He couldn't remember hearing anyone speak above a whisper while traversing this expanse. Naturally Piper proved the exception.

''You haven't lost your touch, I see.'' Her voice invaded the far recesses of the corridor, chasing away the shadows. ''Always the master at creating an impression.''

He inclined his head. ''I do my best.''

''I don't know why you bother, Gideon. You're impressive enough all on your own.''

The observation caught him by surprise. ''A compliment?''

''Fact,'' she responded crisply. ''You have presence. You always have, even as a boy.''

He didn't know how to respond to her comment, so

he lapsed into a remote silence. This meeting wasn't going the way he'd planned, perhaps because he hadn't planned it. At the end of the hallway stood a pair of large double oak doors, stained to a forbidding darkness. He knew how daunting they looked. He'd designed it that way. Piper must have suddenly realized he was still holding her. Sidestepping his arm, she put a discreet distance between them. Her actions irritated him, though he couldn't say why. Over the years he'd become accustomed to people keeping their distance. But coming from her, he found it inexplicably annoying.

Thrusting open the massive doors, he once again clamped an arm around her waist and ushered her across the threshold. And once again she twisted loose and turned to face him. He slammed the doors closed, the sound renting the stillness like a shotgun blast. But aside from an intense wariness that flickered through her gaze, she didn't react with alarm. Rather her expression turned even more combative.

He had to give her credit. Piper Montgomery rarely flinched when confronted with adversity. He liked that. He liked that she wouldn't go down easily. Their battle would be a more equal one, not that it would change the ending. It had taken five years for him to catch her brother, Spencer, at a vulnerable moment in his life and now that he had, Gideon intended to take full advantage.

Piper didn't immediately attack, as she had earlier. Instead she stood in front of him, quietly assimilating the nuances of both the room and the man. To his surprise, she didn't reach for her camera. But then, she'd never used it as a crutch, never attempted to hide behind its all-seeing lens. Piper had always been too vital for that, too involved in life. Rather, she'd wielded it like a

sword of truth, cutting through pretense in order to bare
the reality of any given situation. But perhaps this was
one situation she preferred not to bare. The results might
prove disastrous for both her and Spencer.

Piper offered a cocky smile. "Well? Who goes first?"
She gestured for him to begin. "You, I think."

He didn't need to ask the most obvious question—
why she'd come. They both knew the answer to that.
There were other more interesting issues to deal with.
"Didn't you learn your lesson the last time you put yourself between me and your brother?" he offered as a gentle opening volley.

His comment hit hard and Piper felt the color bleaching from her face as it had in the boardroom when he'd
warned against fighting other people's battles. She struggled for control, using every ounce of self-possession not
to flinch. Unable to continue facing him and also main-
tain an air of calm, she crossed to a squat antique cabinet
Gideon used to conceal electronic equipment. She suspected the uncharacteristic retreat would rouse his hunt-
ing instincts, but that couldn't be helped. She needed
some breathing space.

"Nice," she murmured.

Sure enough, he came after her. "I said something
wrong. What?"

"Is it a Chippendale?"

"That's twice now you've overreacted when I referred to the fight I had with Spencer. I want to know
why."

"It's not a pleasant memory."

"It's not a pleasant memory for either of us. But that
doesn't explain why you look like you're going to faint

whenever I mention it. That's not like you. Now what the hell's going on?''

How could he ask such a question? Had he truly become so heartless that he'd completely lost the capacity to feel? Or did he think time healed all wounds? She fought an uncharacteristic wave of bitterness. He should know that wounds of that magnitude never healed. Not really. Sure, the pain eased, but the ache remained, buried deep where the chance of it being hit by careless words or actions was remote.

She gave her full attention to a dark scar marring the door of the cabinet. She'd hoped her own scars were less obvious, but then, she hadn't taken Gideon's powers of observation into consideration. He'd found that deep, dark place with distressing ease. ''I didn't realize you'd acquired an interest in antiques,'' she said with dogged determination.

To her relief, he allowed the change in subject. No doubt he'd return to the previous topic, but the temporary reprieve allowed her time to recover her composure. ''I'm not interested,'' he claimed. ''I acquired this piece when I picked up Ramsey Industrial.''

She sensed he hadn't offered the comment as an offhand remark. There was a point to his supplying her with the information. Typical. He wasn't a man prone to idle conversation. ''I didn't know you owned them.''

''I don't. They don't exist as a company anymore. They're now part of half a dozen different corporations.''

For some reason his description made her think of a jigsaw puzzle, the pieces broken apart and carelessly tossed into the wrong boxes. Those pieces would never again form a complete whole. Nor would they fit the new puzzle they'd been added to. She ran a finger along the elegant curves of the polished mahogany. The thought saddened her and her mouth tilted into a wry smile. It was a silly reaction, she acknowledged. She didn't have a personal connection to either the company or the people involved.

"So this cabinet is all that's left of Ramsey," she observed.

He shrugged. "I suppose you could say that."

She risked a quick glance in Gideon's direction. She'd spent the last twenty minutes doing her level best to remain unaffected by him, to hold the memories of their time together at a safe distance. Closeted with him in an office that formed the base of his operations made it all the more difficult, particularly after the kiss they'd shared. She couldn't hope to escape his influence, not when they were alone together. Sheer masculine power radiated from him, seemingly amplified by the room, as though his essence had invaded every nook and cranny. The thought was an intimidating one, but no more so than the man, himself.

The years hadn't treated him well, she decided. He'd always had an edgy appearance, his features boldly hewn into formidable peaks and hollows. But now they'd settled into a harsh remoteness warning that he'd given free rein to the darker aspects that shaded his personality. Where once laugh lines had eased the intensity of his dark eyes and stubborn jaw, now she couldn't see any sign of the gentler qualities she'd known so well.

He'd cloaked himself in the civilized appearance of a businessman, but Piper knew better. A tailor-made silk suit and tamed black hair may have replaced his jeans and T-shirt and unruly dark waves, yet there lived a primitive soul beneath the surface polish. It glittered in the fierceness of his gaze and the tautness of a body forged into corded steel by years of hard manual labor. Simple outward trappings couldn't hide the truth. This was a man made ruthless by circumstance, a man who lived without compromise or compassion, perhaps because he'd received so little of either in his youth.

There was another truth she couldn't hide from, no matter how hard she tried. She'd had a hand in creating the austere man Gideon had become. She'd failed him at the most crucial moment in his life. She hadn't been strong enough to fight on his behalf and as a result three people had lost everything they'd held most dear. Not that the knowledge changed anything. The past couldn't be altered. But she could change Gideon's plans for the future. Before she'd been too weak. Now she had both the will and gritty determination necessary to do battle.

Besides, she didn't just owe Spence for what had happened all those years ago. She owed Gideon, as well. It was up to her to set right a terrible wrong. And she would, regardless of the personal price she'd ultimately pay. The only question was how to go about it.

A distinctive stirrup vessel held a place of honor on top of the cabinet and she picked it up in an attempt to give herself time to think, not the least surprised to see it was a genuine artifact. It was a gorgeous ceramic piece of a kneeling warrior painted in red and white slip. If memory served, it had been made to hold and serve liquids. "When did you acquire an interest in pre-Columbian artwork? Or aren't you interested in collecting this, either?"

"I'm not interested. That particular piece belonged to Archibald Fenzer."

Her brow wrinkled in thought. "I've heard that name. Didn't he have something to do with steel? I seem to recall reading he went belly-up a few years back."

Gideon stroked the curve of the warrior's battle club, careful to avoid contact with her hand. Was it deliberate? Did he avoid her touch because he didn't trust himself? She instantly dismissed the thought. If that were the case, he'd never have kissed her.

"Fenzer refused to sell his firm," he explained. "Bankruptcy was his only alternative."

"That's not much of an alternative."

Gideon shrugged. "He preferred it to selling out to me."

Oh, dear. "And did you buy the bits and pieces of his business at the bankruptcy auction?"

"No. It wasn't worth bothering with by then."

She was missing something here. "I don't understand. You bought his artwork, right? Why would you do that if—"

"It was his favorite piece." He carefully took the stirrup vessel from her hand and returned it to the top of the cabinet. "And it serves as a good reminder."

"For you?"

"No."

The answer clicked and she struggled not to reveal her alarm. "You keep it as a reminder for people in a similar position to Mr. Fenzer." He didn't confirm her guess, but she knew she'd gotten it right. "Does it work? Are people more unnerved when you tell them the history behind the piece?"

"We'll find out, won't we?"

She eyed the artifact with distaste. If it didn't have such historic value, she'd see to it that the thing met with an unfortunate dusting accident. Turning, she surveyed his office once again, seeing it in a whole new light. She reached for her camera, curious as to whether her photos would ultimately confirm her suspicions. "Is the entire place decorated from the ravages of other lives, Gideon?" she asked as she set up her shots.

His mouth tightened at her phrasing. "The pieces come from the various companies I've owned."

"Owned…or destroyed?"

"I don't destroy the businesses I buy." A dangerous edge cut through his voice, one she couldn't mistake. "The owners have already done that. I simply pick up the remains at a reasonable price."

She swung around to face him. "And do what with them, Gideon? What happens to the leftovers you collect?"

"I sell them."

There was no reason to get upset. He only confirmed what she'd suspected. "I see. So instead of constructing things as you once did, you deconstruct."

He allowed amusement to override his irritation. "Is that even a word?"

"I'd say you've made it one."

His shoulders shifted beneath his suit jacket, warning of his growing impatience. "We've gotten off the subject."

"No, Gideon. I think we're very much on the subject. You must know I've come about Spence and the contract."

"I figured out that much." A cold pride lent steel to his gaze. "There isn't any other reason you'd come to see me, is there?"

He wouldn't believe the truth, so she didn't bother offering it. "What are your plans?" she asked instead.

His mouth curved into a smile that was a mere ruin of the one she'd once known so intimately. "I plan to deconstruct your brother, of course."

"That contract wasn't with you, Gideon." She forced herself not to plead. She'd never change his mind that way. Years ago she'd have been able to reason with him. But he no longer struck her as reasonable. Too much time had passed and too many hard feelings remained unsettled between them. She knew a man bent on vengeance when she saw one. Hadn't she watched her brother these past five years? "Spence made that agreement with an old family friend."

Gideon nodded. "Jack Wiley. Unfortunately for you, Jack didn't make arrangements to terminate the contract upon his death. Since he didn't, the contract became part of the assets of his estate and came into my possession when I bought Wiley's business from his heirs."

"That wasn't Jack's intention," she attempted to explain. "He was trying to help Spence."

"As I said... He should have made a contingency plan if he didn't want to leave your brother vulnerable."

"So now you're going to call the contract due?"

To her surprise, Gideon shook his head. "Not at all. I simply won't renew it when it expires next month."

Anger flared. "There's a difference?"

"There's a big difference. If I called the contract due now, your brother wouldn't have any options. Giving him an extra month, he can choose how he prefers to go down."

"Generous of you."

Her sarcasm had him closing the distance between

them. "Trust me. I'm being more than generous." His voice lashed the still, ominous air with barely suppressed fury. "Your brother did his level best to destroy me. Did you really think I'd let that go, that I wouldn't find a way to pay him back for his kindness?"

"It wasn't deliberate."

"No? I think he saw it as the perfect excuse to separate us. And he succeeded, didn't he?"

More than Spence's accusations had separated them, as Gideon knew darn well. "And because of what happened over five years ago you intend to destroy him?" she demanded.

"Will losing what he's spent the past five years building destroy Spencer?"

"Yes."

Gideon didn't relent. As far as she could tell there wasn't a hint of compassion or forgiveness. Had those qualities been completely driven from him? "Then maybe he'll feel a small portion of what I did. We'll also see if he has what it takes to pick himself up and move on, or if he'll give up."

"And live his life in bitterness?"

A hint of genuine amusement touched Gideon's expression. "Is that what you think I've done?"

"I think you've allowed bitterness to change the man you once were."

"Not bitterness, sweetheart. Try the hard facts of life." And every last one of those hard facts scored his face. "You and your brother put me on this path. Why act surprised when you discover I've followed it?"

Piper shook her head. "Don't blame us for what you've become. We make our own choices in life, Gideon." She turned to examine his office once again.

It was tragic to think he'd built his foundation atop the ashes of devastation. How many different firms did all this represent? How many ghosts haunted the various bits and pieces? "Don't you regret any of what you've done?"

He took a stance directly behind her. "I only have one regret in life."

"Which is?"

His hands closed on her shoulders, turning her around to face him. "You haven't earned the right to know."

That roused her curiosity. "Earned?"

All expression vanished from his face and it struck Piper that she'd never sensed such loneliness in a man before. It revealed a vulnerability he'd never have acknowledged. Nor would he appreciate having her pick up on it. She ached to hold him, to ease his pain as she had when they'd been together. But that was beyond her abilities. He'd never allow her to get that close. Not again. Once upon a time he'd have accepted her embrace. But now he'd see it as a weakness, a weakness in need of serious defense measures.

"Years ago I confided my childish secrets to you," he said.

"I haven't forgotten." She regarded him steadily. "But you seem to have."

"They were foolish dreams. Pointless dreams."

"And the goals you've replaced them with are better?"

"Yes."

"Why?"

"Because no one can take away what I have."

This time she did laugh, the sound edged with sorrow. "Oh, Gideon. No one can take what you possess because you haven't built anything worthy of that. And they can't touch you personally because you won't let them close enough to hurt you again.''

''Nor will I.'' His implacability only served to confirm her suspicions. No doubt it would make her job all the more difficult. ''Let's get this over with, Piper. You've done your duty. You've come to plead with me on your brother's behalf. And I've rejected your pleas. Go home and tell Spencer that it's time to pay for what he did.''

She shook her head with a stubbornness that matched his. ''No, Gideon. I'm not here to beg for mercy. Far from it.''

''Don't hand me that. You're here about the contract.''

''You're right. I am.''

He lifted a sooty eyebrow. ''Have you come to fulfill the terms?''

''Yes.''

Surprise, along with an intense irritation turned his eyes to ebony. ''The terms are to either repay the loan or turn over Spencer's property. You don't have the kind of money it would take to pay back the loan. I've checked.''

''No, we don't.''

''Then you plan to negotiate my takeover of the mill?''

''You're forgetting the third alternative.''

It didn't take long for him to come up with their other choice. ''You have collateral of equal value to offer?''

She didn't hesitate. ''Yes, I do.''

"I'm warning you, Piper. I expect my money's worth."

"Oh, you'll get it."

"What are you going to give me?"

She smiled. "Myself. I'm the collateral on the loan."

CHAPTER TWO

FURY ripped through Gideon. "Is this some sort of joke?"

Piper shook her head, impervious to his anger. "Not at all."

"Let me get this straight. You're offering yourself as collateral for Spencer's loan?"

"What's the matter, Gideon? Don't you think I'm worth it?"

If she knew how close to the edge he was, she wouldn't taunt him. She'd be running flat-out for the nearest exit. "You don't want to know what I'm thinking right now," he warned.

"You were the one who taught me to tackle problems creatively."

She tilted her head to one side, her hair flowing across her shoulder. More than anything he longed to thrust his hands into that silken curtain as he'd done so often when they'd been lovers. His fingers itched to know that distinctive texture again. The opportunity he'd had in the boardroom had only whetted his appetite without coming anywhere close to sating it, and the craving had grown so intense it had become a physical ache. Of course, his weakness only added to his frustration, forcing him to acknowledge how much power she could still wield over him.

"Tackle problems creatively?" he repeated. "What the hell are you talking about, Piper?"

''Don't you remember?'' An eager warmth gleamed in her eyes. Why did she have to be so damn enticing? It drove him crazy. He'd like to be able to dismiss her, to toss her out of his office without a second thought. Instead, every testosterone-driven instinct urged him to lock the doors and keep her. *Keep her.* The words carried a primitive directive that held infinite appeal. ''You once told me that when you didn't have the money to purchase what you wanted, you had to find a creative alternative.''

''Forget it,'' he retorted. ''I'm not buying.''

Her chin took on a defiant set. ''I'm not asking you to buy. I'm worth more than that contract. I haven't been idle these past five years. I can be a huge asset to you and your firm.''

''Doing what? Taking pictures?''

He hadn't asked the question sarcastically. He respected her abilities. She'd started building a name as a baby photographer when they'd been together, her black-and-white photos capturing unforgettable images that had won her instant local acclaim, even at the tender age of twenty.

She shrugged. ''If photos are what you want, I'm happy to accommodate you. Actually I thought my administrative abilities might be of more value. I have a degree in business management, in addition to my photographic skills. Or failing that, I'm excellent with people. I always have been. Perhaps personnel has an opening.''

''Not a chance.''

An uncustomary grimness settled over her features, the expression sitting oddly on the delicate curves. She'd always been someone who offered a quick laugh, who smoothed over troubles rather than stirring them to a boil. But he'd forgotten how stubborn she could be, particularly in the face of adversity. When she decided to confront a problem, she did it without hesitation or compromise, and with a passion that couldn't be deflected.

"I'm not offering you a choice," she informed him. "I'm telling you that under the terms of the contract it's *our* decision, mine and Spence's. He can either give up the mill, repay the money Jack loaned him or offer collateral of equal value to the amount fronted him. We're selecting the final option."

"And I'm refusing it."

She inclined her head. "That's also your option, in which case the contract is null and void. I suggest you reread the pertinent passages, Gideon. You'll find you don't have any alternatives."

"There are always alternatives."

"Is that what you told the owners of all the companies you've taken over? Did you encourage them to find alternative solutions to the one you were offering?"

He didn't attempt to deny the truth. "Of course I didn't."

To his surprise she didn't respond with either satisfaction or triumph at his admission. Rather, a hint of compassion colored her words. "Think about it, Gideon. If you refuse to renew the contract, we have no choice but to fulfill the terms."

"That's the whole idea."

"Fine. But Spence and I are still left with three options available to us, including choosing collateral of equal value." Her expression turned downright mischievous. "Which means you're stuck with me."

Gideon paced in an effort to walk off his frustration.

She hadn't changed one damn bit. She was digging in like the most ornery mule, the same as she'd always done. Sure, she was being pleasant about it, but that didn't change the end result. More times than not her stubbornness caused her greater harm than anyone else. This occasion would prove no exception. Didn't she see that? "I find it hard to believe that Spencer agreed to this. He always preferred fighting his own battles. Or is he hoping you can change my mind?"

Piper shook her head. "We both know that isn't going to happen. Spence understands all about revenge, just as he understands what you and I once had is dead and buried."

"If he understands about revenge, why send you?" He swung around to face her. "Why put you in harm's way? That isn't like him."

Something in her expression gave him pause. It wasn't often that Piper refused to meet his eyes. She had an innate honesty and directness that hadn't changed any more than her obstinacy. Then it clicked. "Dammit, Piper! He doesn't know what you're up to, does he?"

An impudent smile crept across the generous curves of her mouth and she shrugged. "Spence can be almost as stubborn as you. Since he's out of town right now, I decided this was one of those occasions that might be better presented as a done deal rather than an option subject to further discussion."

"Oh, there's going to be further discussion. Count on it."

Her smile faded and a fierce determination took hold. "We're not turning this into another battle like the one you staged in your boardroom."

"I assure you that wasn't staged."

"You put it into motion and did nothing to stop it from escalating. I'd say that was as close to staging something as you can get."

He lifted an eyebrow. "Are you blaming me because the various owners and representatives of those three jewelry firms couldn't control themselves?"

"Is that what they are? Jewelers?" She nodded. "Yes, absolutely. I blame you for putting people in an untenable situation, one guaranteed to bring out the worst in them. It was deliberate. You know it. I know it. And once those men and women have a chance to sober up, calm down and reflect, they'll know it, too."

"Enough, Piper. There's a limit to how much I'll take."

"Oh, I haven't begun to have my say," she retorted fiercely. "You were once a man I respected more than any in the whole of Mill Run. But you've changed. You're not that man anymore."

Gideon's control vanished, ripped from him with stunning ease by a few careless words from a woman he'd once loved and valued more than anything in his life, even his precious word of honor. "That man doesn't exist anymore! He was torn apart piece by piece until there was nothing left."

"That's an excuse. You can rise above adversity. Isn't that what you always told me?" She made the mistake of approaching. Worse, she put her hands on him. Soft hands. Gentle hands. Loving hands. "You always said that outside influences don't make the man. You said that with drive and determination and by keeping one's word, a person could overcome any hardship."

"A child told you that. A foolish child who hadn't learned the hard, cold facts of life."

"And what facts are those?"

He stared at the fingers clutching his arm. They were so pale, so delicate and feminine against the darkness of his suit. Did she have any sense of her own vulnerability? Did she have any clue how easily he could crush the vibrancy of her spirit? She couldn't or she wouldn't be here. No one was that self-sacrificing. She'd be finding the deepest, darkest hole to hide in until he'd expended his wrath over Spencer's bullheaded skull.

Very gently he removed her hand from his arm. It was either that or give in to the urges that had been clawing at him since she'd first burst through the boardroom door. "The fact is that money and power are the only currency people understand or accept. No one gives a damn about truth, let alone drive and determination. My word of honor meant nothing all those years ago. When put to the test, the people of Mill Run were only too happy to believe the accusations leveled by the town's leading citizens against the son of a drunk."

"How would you know?" she shot back. "You and Spence fought that day and then you took off, leaving havoc behind. How is anyone supposed to believe you when you didn't stick around long enough to stand by your word of honor? Spence told me—"

"*Don't!*" The word exploded from him and it took a full minute to rein in his fury. He lowered his voice, the softness more deadly than anything he might have said in anger. "If you value your life, do *not* quote your brother to me."

"Gideon—"

He flashed her a warning look that checked whatever she'd intended to say. "Enough of this nonsense, Piper. All that was over long ago. Forget the past and deal with the present. We have business to take care of and I suggest we get on with it.''

''Since I'm just collateral, I guess I'm not in a position to argue.'' She cast him a disgruntled scowl. ''Much.''

He cut loose with a word that brought hot color to her cheeks. Tugging at his tie, he yanked at the stranglehold it had on his neck while fighting to recover his temper. How the hell did she manage to get him riled up so easily? His reputation for icy calm was renowned throughout the business community and yet all she had to do was open her mouth to break his control. The irony wasn't lost on him.

''I give you full credit for inventiveness,'' he finally said. ''But that doesn't change a thing. Your brother signed a contract with Jack Wiley and I'm collecting what's owed. Whether that's now or in one month doesn't matter in the least. Spencer's going down and you'd be smart to get out of the way.''

He thought she might waver, that his anger might have been enough to scare her off. But he'd underestimated her. Taking a deep breath, she held her ground, resolution burning in her eyes. ''You're collecting what's owed you right now. And I'm it. As I said, reread the pertinent clauses. You can't refuse my offer, Gideon, not unless you intend to void the contract. I'm the collateral on the loan, which means I'm all yours.''

''Interesting phrasing.''

Still, she didn't back down. ''Collateral isn't worth anything unless it offers full value for your money.''

He should refuse her offer, but the more he considered, the more tempted he was to accept. That one kiss had told him a lot. He wanted Piper as desperately today as he'd wanted her five years ago. It had been too long

since he'd held her in his arms. Kissed her as he had in
the boardroom. Taken her to his bed and made her his.
Perhaps his revenge against Spencer would prove
sweeter than he'd anticipated. He could accept Piper's
offer. He'd be a fool not to. Then, when the workload
became too much and she walked out, he'd call the loan
due. And in the process, he'd have taken back all that
Spencer had stolen from him.

"You're sure you're willing to do this?" he pressed.
"I'm not going to make it easy on you."

Amusement resurfaced in her gaze. "It never occurred
to me that you would."

"You understand that if your value doesn't match
what I'd have realized from the repayment of the loan
that nothing you do or say will save your brother?"

"You've made that painfully clear."

"Let me make something else painfully clear." Two
swift steps returned him to her side and he drew her into
his arms. "The minute I accept your offer, you're going
to become my everything. All I want, all I ask, all I
demand, you'll do."

"I understand when it comes to business, I'm yours."
Her body relaxed into his, as though some unconscious
part of her trusted him implicitly. Gideon's mouth tightened. She was foolish to reveal so much, especially to a
man like him. "But you'll have to respect the boundaries
between a business obligation and more personal demands."

He gave in to overwhelming desire and slid his hands
into her hair. He could feel his inner tension loosen, as
though her touch had the ability to soothe the demons
that drove him. At the same time, touching her provoked
a new source of tension, a craving that was fast becom-

ing more and more difficult to resist. "What if my demands involve both?"

"I'm collateral on a business loan, not a personal one." Piper met his eyes with an unwavering gaze, her certainty stirring memories of long-ago events when her faith in him had been absolute. "I know you'll respect that, Gideon, that you won't use our business situation to force something more."

But he wanted that something more. He wanted all she had to give. Not that he'd take it with force. He hadn't fallen that far from grace. "In all the years I've known you, I've never treated you with anything other than respect."

She carefully untangled herself from his arms. "Then don't start now."

The loss of physical contact hit harder than he cared to admit. "This isn't going to work, Piper."

"Why? Because you can't stand the idea of working with me?" She tilted her head to one side. "Or is it that you're concerned you might like it too much?"

He went perfectly still, shoving out a warning from between clenched teeth. "Get out now, while you still have the chance."

She winced. "Pushed the wrong button, did I?"

"You might avoid that one in the future."

"Fair enough. I'll go." She took a step away from him. Then another. "But I'll be back first thing in the morning."

"I suggest you reconsider that decision."

"I can't."

"Because of Spence."

"No, Gideon." She crossed to the door of the office. If circumstances had been different he'd have laughed at the way she had to tug to get them open. But all thought of humor died when she turned and added, "I'll be back because you need me."

Piper leaned against the closed doors to Gideon's office and fought to draw breath. She'd done it. She'd actually faced him after all these years and lived to tell the tale. True, she'd picked up another few bruises. But they were minor compared to the ones he'd left five years ago.

Heaven help her, how Gideon had changed. She could barely find any remnants of the man she'd once known. He'd all but vanished and that undeniable fact devastated her more than she cared to admit. He'd always been hard, bearing his scars with a stoic resolve that nearly broke her heart. But that hardness had been tempered by a compassion and generosity she'd witnessed from her earliest years. Defender of the underdog, nemesis of bullies, protector, warrior, lover. He'd been all those things and more. But she'd never have guessed him capable of such virtues based on the man she'd met today. His anger lingered too close to the surface, oddly volcanic, his wounds still fresh, even after five full years.

Straightening, she discovered that her legs would actually hold her now and she headed down the endless hallway toward the exit. The artificial hush seemed more daunting this time around, perhaps because she felt a bit more emotionally battered than earlier. She paused outside the doorway leading to the boardroom, wondering if she should return the way she'd come or search for a different exit. Faint voices penetrated the thick wood, taking the choice from her hands. Unable to resist meddling, she entered.

The vestiges of chaos remained, the boardroom a total

disaster. It would take quite a while to get the place back into usable shape. Gideon's little surprise was going to cost a pretty penny in redecoration expenses. Other than the caterer, no one had left yet, the representatives of the various jewelry companies milling around in small, nervous clumps looking decidedly anxious.

"Good afternoon," she said, closing the door behind her. Every last one turned toward her as though she offered imminent salvation. It gave her an idea. "Could you all take a seat, please? I have a few questions I'd like to ask."

Gideon stood in the middle of his office, silently cursing beneath his breath. How did she manage to do it? How did she manage to break through barriers he'd spent years fortifying? With one simple smile she'd nearly brought him to his knees. It was ridiculous. He was the one with the power. Didn't she realize that?

He grimaced, running a hand across his nape. No. She didn't and never had.

Piper Montgomery had a knack for remaining as oblivious to the shoulds and oughts of the world as she remained oblivious to her own vulnerability. She'd always been that way, even as a child. He remembered the first time he'd seen that quality in her. She'd been all of seven or eight and had been standing in front of the candy counter at Murphy's Newsstand, considering her options with the air of a serious chocolate connoisseur. Gideon had also been known to give candy similar attention. The difference between them was that she could afford to buy whatever appealed and he couldn't.

He remembered lounging against a stand overflowing with comic books and watching her, a cocky hellion about to rack up his first teenage year. Of course, he recognized her. Miss Montgomery Mansion, he and his friends called her. She was always dressed with pristine perfection, pulling off what would have been a social disaster in anyone else, with a panache he could recognize, if not name.

There was something about her, he was forced to admit, something that elicited a grudging admiration. Fearless blue eyes confronted the world in a way he secretly envied, even her stance one of absolute defiance. Of course, she could get away with being both fearless and defiant. She was in a different class from Gideon Garbage, her hilltop home as far removed from his rusted-out trailer as it was possible to get. Everything about her reinforced that distinction.

She carried herself like a princess, the dance classes she took doing weird things to the way she walked. Maybe it was because she never walked. She flitted or danced or skipped or twirled. Even when she was in a line at school where everyone had been ordered to stand still, she remained in constant motion, her pale blond head bobbing like the colorful float attached to his fishing line.

She leaned closer to the candy counter and her pale blond hair flowed forward to curtain her face. It was longer and straighter than any other girl's in school. He'd often joked with his friends that her parents wouldn't let her out of the house until they'd made sure that every single strand had been measured and razor-cut to the exact same length. She was cute enough, for a kid, he supposed. Plenty cuter than the brats his mother routinely turned out. And she couldn't help how her parents dressed her, her scrawny arms and legs poking out from beneath a laughable amount of lace and gut-churning pastels. Fact was, her cheerful attitude usually made him smile, a feat that impressed him more than anything else about her.

Staring for so long at the candy made Gideon's stomach grumble and he knew it was time to push off. As much as he'd like to drool over Murphy's selection, he'd have to satisfy his unending hunger with the single bar tucked in his pocket. Besides, he had better things to do than stand around staring at some rich kid—like going by the old mill and snagging a string of trout for dinner.

He pushed off from the comic book stand and headed for the exit. If he didn't have better luck than yesterday, his family would be stuck with franks and beans for dinner again. And anything was better than that, especially since the number of available dogs rarely matched the number of demanding mouths.

"Hey, you! Hart." Gideon had just reached the door when a heavy hand dropped on his shoulder and spun him around. "Where do you think you're going?" the owner of the store demanded.

"I'm leaving, of course. What does it look like?" Gideon attempted to shrug off Murphy's restraining hand. "What's your problem, man?"

"My problem is you." A stubby finger stabbed him in the chest. "You're a damn thief. You're trying to sneak out of my store without paying for your candy."

"What the hell are you talking about?"

"Watch your mouth, boy." Florid color swept into his heavy face. "You're just like your old man. Blood will tell, you know. I should have thrown you out when you first came in here."

"Get off me." Gideon wriggled beneath the crushing

hold. Not that it helped. Murphy was one of the biggest, beefiest men in town. "I didn't steal anything."

"That candy bar you've got sticking out of your pocket. You didn't pay for it."

The accusation infuriated Gideon. "Bull. I paid your kid for it. Go ask him."

He glanced at Murphy's son and saw from the smirk on the kid's face that he'd get no help from that quarter. His shouted obscenity didn't help his situation, earning him a swift smack upside his head.

"Call the sheriff, son," Murphy ordered. He grabbed Gideon by the ear, preventing him from running, the old man's grip tight enough to provoke tears. Not that Gideon would ever let them fall. Hell, no. He'd sooner slit his own throat. "It's past time this punk gets his first view from behind a pair of bars. Not that it'll be his last. No sirree, it sure as hell won't be his last. Like father, like son."

"Let him go!"

Gideon would never forget the look of astonishment on Murphy's face when Piper came charging over. She didn't walk. She didn't flit. She didn't dance or skip or twirl. She flew. And she didn't stop until she was right on top of them, a tiny whirlwind of fury that came no higher than the store owner's overflowing girth. Even more astonishing, she smacked Murphy's huge paw of a hand, the one with a death grip on Gideon's ear. It couldn't have stung more than a mosquito bite, yet he jerked his hand back as though his fingers had been set on fire and took a hasty step away from Piper.

"What are you doin', girl?" Murphy's question was more complaint than demand.

She took up a stance directly in front of Gideon,

spreading her scrawny arms wide, as though her bony little willow twigs had a chance of fending off Murphy's gnarled oak trees. "Gideon Hart did so pay for that candy bar. I saw him. He gave Timmy a quarter, three dimes and a nickel." She turned her blazing blue eyes on the hapless son. "And if you say he didn't, then you're a liar."

It was the funniest thing Gideon had ever seen and he further confounded Murphy by busting into laughter. At least it helped dispel the tears of pain he'd been so desperately blinking back. "You tell 'em, pipsqueak," he encouraged gruffly.

"My daddy always said a man's word of honor is the most important thing he has. Gideon said he paid and he did. That's what word of honor means, always telling the truth no matter what. All the kids say that Gideon never fibs." A hint of awe colored her words. "Not ever."

It was then that Spencer walked into the store. A couple of years older than Gideon, he sized up the situation with a single look. "Problem?" he asked mildly.

To Gideon's astonishment, Piper didn't rush to her brother's side as he'd half expected. She didn't burst into tears or beg for help or react in any of the ways most girls would have. Instead she held her stance, her gaze never shifting from Murphy's son. "Tell the truth," she ordered. "Tell your daddy Gideon paid."

Timmy wilted beneath her blazing regard. "He paid," the boy muttered.

Murphy exploded, no doubt from sheer embarrassment. "Out. All of you get out of here."

None of them wasted any time. The three were through the door in two seconds flat. Even Spencer moved with impressive speed. Gideon stood with them on the sidewalk, not quite sure what to do or say next. Shoving his hand into his pocket, he yanked out the candy bar he'd bought and thrust it into Piper's face. "Here."

She shook her head, politely refusing his offer. That might have been the end of it, but her perfectly straight hair caught in an errant breeze and whipped around his arm, shackling him. He'd never felt anything so soft in his entire life and he utilized a gentleness he didn't realize he possessed to pick the strands free and smooth them into order.

The instant he'd freed her, he offered the candy bar again, his discomfort making his words harsher than he'd intended. "Take it, I said."

"No, thank you," she repeated in her best Miss Montgomery Mansion tone of voice.

Gideon could feel his face reddening. Spencer still hadn't said anything, which only made matters worse. Did he think Piper was wrong? Did he believe she'd rescued a liar and a thief? Probably. People tended to suspect the worst of him. "You earned it." He shook the candy bar in front of Piper's nose, deliberately infusing his voice with a hint of impatience, as though what had happened hadn't meant a thing to him. "Come on, pipsqueak. Take it. You didn't get to buy a candy for yourself."

She hesitated for another second, then took the bar and neatly snapped it in half. "We'll share it. That's fair, right?"

"Fair." He must have stared at her outstretched hand for a full thirty seconds. Did she have to be so nice, act so friggin' sympathetic? Like he was a charity case, or something. He didn't know how to respond other than with all the careless disdain an adolescent boy could muster. "Yeah, whatever."

He'd hurt her, he could tell from the way her eyes went all flat and dark. And it made him feel smaller than anything Murphy could have said or done. Spencer dropped his arm around his sister's shoulders in a protective gesture. "Come on, Piper. Let's go." He didn't give her a chance to argue, but turned her toward home. "Next time fight your own battles," he threw over his shoulder as a parting shot.

Gideon stood motionless on the sidewalk for a whole five seconds before going after them. It took every ounce of nerve he possessed to brush Spencer aside and confront Piper. "I forgot to say thanks."

"That's okay."

"No, it's not," he insisted doggedly. "You stood up for me when no one else would have. Timmy wouldn't have told the truth if you hadn't made him. And I won't forget that. If any of the kids at school say anything bad about you, they've got me to answer to."

"She already has a brother," Spencer interrupted. "She doesn't need anyone else defending her."

Gideon refused to back down. "Tough. She's got me now. Nobody's gonna hurt her. Not nobody." He met her eyes, stunned to see something that looked remarkably like hero worship gleaming there. "You have my word of honor."

From that day on, the phrase became his personal motto.

Whenever anyone doubted him, he'd stick to his guns and repeat Piper's words over and over until he'd convinced each and every last person of his sincerity. And he made sure he backed up what he said, internalizing the true intent behind the expression, externalizing it, eating, drinking and sleeping the concept inherent in her statement until it formed the very core of who and what he was.

That boy survived for more than ten years, a boy from a run-down trailer park on the wrong side of town whose word of honor was his most valuable possession—his only possession. It forged the man he became, a man who fought for his dignity with callused hands and a sturdy back and an uncompromising work ethic. And it lasted right up until a fateful day beside the smoldering ruins of a hundred-year-old mill when he realized that the words he'd honored for so long were just that. Words. They meant nothing. They had achieved nothing. They were worth nothing. And they never would be.

Gideon stared at the huge double doors that separated him from Piper. What the hell had she meant? *I'll be back because you need me.* He didn't need anyone. He hadn't for a long time. Need came from vulnerability and he'd worked long and hard to strip himself of all vulnerability. But apparently, there was one he'd neglected to rid himself of, one he'd have plenty of opportunity to eliminate over the coming month.

A vulnerability named Piper.

CHAPTER THREE

"GOOD morning, Gideon." Piper smiled at the man she'd once loved more than life itself. It was a smile that seemed to emanate from the deepest part of her being and she could no more control it than she could explain why she'd still feel such an intense connection to him after all these years. "Ready to get to work?"

He didn't even look up from the papers scattered across his desk. "I believe that's my line."

Her smile widened. "Then I've already answered it, haven't I? I'm ready, willing and able to—how did you put it?—be your everything."

That caught his attention. His head jerked up and something dark and hungry flickered within his gaze. "Dangerous words, Piper."

"They were your words, Gideon. You said them to me just yesterday. Don't you remember?"

The hungry gleam became more pronounced. "I remember they put you into a flat-out panic."

"Don't be ridiculous," she scoffed. "It takes more than mere words to panic me."

"How about actions?" He tossed aside his pen and shoved back his chair. "Would those panic you?"

"They didn't yesterday, now did they?" She'd pushed him far enough. Despite her gentle taunts she really didn't want him turning a business agreement into something more personal. At least, not yet. "What's first on the agenda? Should I report to personnel? I brought

along a résumé, in case. Or have you already decided
where I'm to work?''

"Oh, I've decided.''

The grimness of his voice didn't escape her notice.
She suspected she knew what had caused it, too. She
released her breath in a silent sigh. ''I've given you too
much time to think, haven't I?''

"Come again?''

She perched on the corner of his desk, a desk as oppressive and foreboding as the rest of his office. The man
clearly had something against sweetness and light. One
more problem she'd need to address. ''I said...I've
given you too much time to think. Let's see if this
sounds familiar.'' She tilted her head to one side.
''You've decided you've made a mistake.''

"A big mistake.''

"Right. A big mistake. You should have gone after
Spence directly instead of discussing the contract with
me. You certainly shouldn't have let me talk you into
this collateral nonsense. But most unprofessional of all,
you allowed me to get too close. You kissed me. Me,
your worst enemy.'' She paused, lifting her eyebrows.
''Sound familiar?''

He stood and planted his hands on his desktop, leaning forward until he'd crowded into her personal space.
As an intimidation method, it was very effective. But
not quite effective enough—not if his goal was to force
her retreat. He probably didn't realize that she liked being crowded by him. Now that she thought about it, she
liked it a little too much. She could inhale his crisp,
clean scent until she turned dizzy with it, feel the warmth
of his body lap over her, hear the steady give and take
of his breath. It all sounded and felt and smelled deli-

ciously familiar, like a well-loved treat she hadn't experienced for so long she'd almost forgotten how much she missed it. Now those memories came rushing back, along with a craving so intense she wouldn't be able to resist it for long.

"You have it all figured out, don't you?" he asked.

She forced herself to focus on the problem at hand and ignore everything else. It was quite a feat considering that the "everything else" consisted of Gideon, a man impossible to ignore. "I have some of it figured out." There were still a few missing puzzle pieces that Spencer would need to fill in as soon as he returned from his business meeting in California. "I suspect a detail or two might have escaped my notice."

To her relief, he pulled back. Thrusting his hands into his pockets, he crossed to the windows overlooking the city of Denver. She released her breath in a silent sigh. That was close. A few more seconds and she'd have done something disastrous…like bridge the remaining distance between them and sample a bit of that long-forgotten and well-loved treat.

"This isn't going to work, Piper."

She'd expected him to say that. "It's going to be difficult," she agreed.

"I could sue your brother for the money instead of putting up with all this nonsense."

"You could. But think how much more fun you'll have taking all that pent-up revenge out on me, instead." She gave an exaggerated shiver. "Doesn't the idea of making my life miserable brighten up your day?"

She'd have been happier if he'd categorically denied it, instead of turning to eye her with such predatory interest. "Do you think this is a game?"

His tone worried her. It had become calm and detached, a sure sign that he was feeling the precise opposite. "I haven't decided what it is," she admitted.

"I promise, I'm not playing with you. I also promise if you decide to put yourself in the line of fire, you're going to get hurt."

The words escaped before she could stop them. "I'm used to it, coming from you."

Did he flinch? If so, he recovered swiftly. "I think you have that backward."

Wait a minute. "What's that supposed to mean?" she demanded.

"It means that you and your brother did far greater damage to me than any I might have inflicted on you." He stopped her before she could ask questions, cutting her off with a single sweep of his hand. With his back to the window, she couldn't make out his expression, but his tone was more than enough to guarantee her silence. "Enough, Piper. I suggest you listen to my terms. You can take them or leave them. Personally I don't give a damn. But if you're serious about being Spencer's collateral, you should know what you're agreeing to."

She made herself more comfortable on his desktop, her audacity earning a narrow-eyed glare. "I'm ready. Hit me." She compounded her peril with a cheeky grin. "Figuratively speaking, of course."

"You'll be paid an entry level salary. All of it, after taxes, will go toward repayment of the loan."

"All of it?" That didn't sound right. "You're not going to leave me enough for food or rent?"

"If you need money for living expenses get it from your brother. Or start charging more for your baby pictures."

Uh-oh. She moistened her lips. "I—I don't take baby pictures anymore."

That caught his attention. "You've given it up?" His brow creased in a frown. "Why would you do that? You were good. Really good."

"I've switched to brides and grooms." She managed to make the statement with a nonchalant carelessness, as though it hadn't been one of the most painful decisions she'd ever made. "They're easier to work with."

"I liked the ones you did of babies."

Piper folded her arms across her chest, hoping it didn't make her appear too defensive. "It's not your decision, is it?" She deliberately changed the subject. "So, you're going to keep all of my salary."

He hesitated, as though he'd have liked to continue their previous discussion. Then with a shrug, he confirmed, "Every penny." He fell silent, waiting for her to say something, to protest or complain or argue. There could only be one reason.

She acknowledged his cleverness with a knowing look. "Good try, Gideon, but it's not going to work. You can't get me to change my mind that easily."

"I think it'll work better than you suspect," he warned. "Oh, not at first. You're tenacious. You'll stick it out for a while. But Spence won't let you run yourself into the ground for long before stepping in and giving me what I want. He has too much pride to let his little sister take the fall for his actions."

"You have it all figured, don't you?"

"I want Spencer. One way or another, I'm going to have him."

"We'll see."

Piper stretched across his desk, tidying the papers

within reach in order to give herself time to think. She certainly had her work cut out for her. Not only would she have to find a way to break through the barriers Gideon had built up and free the man she'd once known, but she'd also have to deal with her brother's reaction when he found out how she'd elected to handle the loss of the contract. She shot an uneasy glance toward the windows. Unfortunately Gideon was right.

Spence would do everything within his power to keep her safe from harm, and he'd definitely consider her current predicament—as well as the man responsible for it—harmful to her well-being. With luck, she'd be able to ease her brother's fears long enough to resolve their financial situation before he did something unconscionably noble, like surrendering the mill he'd spent the past five years rebuilding. Addressing all the different problems would be quite a challenge, even for someone as optimistic as she tended to be. But she'd manage.

She had to.

That decided, she returned her attention to Gideon. "Okay, Mr. Hart. I accept your terms." She made certain she didn't betray by word or expression any hesitation or doubt. "Shall we get on with it? What's first on the agenda?"

"You can start by getting off my desk." The order had a bite to it, one she'd be wise to heed. Clearly he'd expected her to refuse his terms. Having crossed him, she could expect him to extract a certain level of retaliation. "Employees stand—or when invited—sit in a chair."

She obediently left his desk and wandered across his office to the antique-topped cabinet. "What's next?"

"Your first assignment is to get together with the

owners of the jewelry companies who were at the board meeting yesterday and admit you lied. Then you're to tell them the truth.''

She glanced over her shoulder. ''And what truth is that?''

''That Hart & Associates will be buying them out and selling off their assets, as I explained at yesterday's meeting. Nothing has changed. You're to make that point very clear. You're not to offer any explanations or reassurances. All questions should be directed to my office.'' He remained standing by the windows, watching her with nerve-racking intensity. Was he hoping she'd balk at this first job? If so, he'd underestimated her. She'd already guessed what he'd ask. ''Since you've given them false hope, it's up to you to correct the situation.''

She returned her attention to the artifact, scowling at it. Darn the thing for being so lovely. She'd have been much happier if it were a misshapen lump of clay instead of rich with the beauty of its heritage. She itched to send the stirrup vessel hooking toward the nearest trash can. ''Just out of curiosity... What items are you going to keep as trophies for deconstructing these new firms?''

''I don't take trophies.''

''Sure you do. Oh, I realize you think they're just bits and pieces salvaged from the companies you've owned.'' She found herself tracing the scar marring the cabinet door, relating to it on some unconscious level. ''But when I developed the pictures I took, they showed something very odd.''

His brows drew together. ''This conversation is a complete waste of time. I suggest we get to work.''

She ignored his dictate, as well as his frown.

Something told her it was an expression that came all too easily to Gideon these days. She'd have to see what she could do about changing that, too. Crossing to her case, she yanked out a handful of black-and-white photographs. She placed them close together on his desk, so they overlapped one another, and gestured for him to join her.

"What is it, Piper?" he demanded impatiently.

"The photos from yesterday." She gave him a minute to study the collage of shots. "It took me a while to realize what was wrong. But then I noticed that none of your furnishings matched. See?" She tapped several of the more obvious ones with her fingernail. "It isn't as apparent when you're standing here looking at the actual pieces. But when they're bunched together like this in a series of pictures, it jumps right out at you."

"Your point?"

Did he really not know? She found that difficult to believe. Very little slipped by Gideon's keen gaze. "There isn't anything here that you selected on your own, is there? I mean that you decided you needed and went out and shopped for. Are any of these items personal choices?"

She didn't think he'd answer. After a moment his mouth compressed into a line and he shook his head in a single abrupt movement. "No."

It took her a second to perceive how wrong she'd been. He *didn't* know. "Oh, Gideon," she whispered, compassion washing over her. "You never even realized these things were trophies, did you?"

"I told you. They're not—" He swore beneath his breath. Knocking a chair from his path, he prowled the length of the room, his tension electrifying the air between them. His black eyes glittered with all he longed to express, but fought to control. "Dammit to hell! How do you do it, Piper? You have the most annoying knack of any woman I've ever known for getting under my skin."

She refused to back down, choosing honesty over discretion despite the risk. "I just notice things you don't want to see."

A hint of self-mockery replaced his anger. "So now you're going to be my conscience, as well as my employee?"

She couldn't resist teasing in the hopes of lightening his mood. He definitely had the look of a man on the edge. "Only if it means double the pay."

"Good try."

She lifted an eyebrow. "But, no?"

"Not a chance in hell."

She shrugged. "In that case, you'll have to be responsible for your own conscience." Abandoning the photos, she returned to the cabinet. It drew her with annoying persistence. Was it the stupid scar? Or were ghostly echoes from a life come and gone calling to her? "I've found that taking pictures helps since they have an uncanny knack for revealing the truth. You might consider giving it a try. You can use my camera, if you'd like."

"I'll pass, thanks." He stopped a few feet away, close enough to spark an uncomfortable awareness and yet, far enough away that she wasn't tempted to embarrass herself with an undignified retreat. "I'm sure your attention to those sorts of details will prove an annoying asset for Hart & Associates."

"I can only hope." She removed the stirrup vessel

from the top of the cabinet and opened one of the cupboard doors. Since she couldn't bring herself to destroy the thing, it gave her more pleasure than she could express to shove it out of sight. "Now I have a question for you. Why did you arrange for the owners of all three companies to get together at the same time?"

"Simple. To tell them I planned to gut their businesses."

"I got that part." Piper turned to discover that he'd halved the distance between them. Oh, dear. She forced herself to take a deep, steadying breath. Tension still gripped him, but there was a difference. The anger had dissipated, leaving behind a new, more disturbing turbulence, a visceral awareness that had nothing to do with business and everything to do with an irresistible, burgeoning want. "What I mean is, why all three at once? You could have done it individually."

"I could have. But this way I ended it with one fast meeting."

Piper gave the matter her full concentration—tough to do with Gideon intent on blistering her with so much masculine energy. It positively radiated from him, burning in his black eyes and tensing the sinuous muscles and tendons that not even a tailored suit coat could fully conceal. "Yet something you said or did caused open warfare. What was it?"

He shifted impatiently. "What difference does it make?"

"Humor me," she encouraged, edging away from the cabinet. It wasn't a retreat. Heavens, no. There was no need for that. "Since I'm the one stuck dealing with the various parties, I'd like all the facts."

"You'll still have to tell everyone the truth," he

warned, following her. Or was he stalking? "I'll even be generous and let you give them the good news one at a time instead of all together, if you prefer."

"And are you also going to send a bodyguard with me?" To heck with a bodyguard for her meetings. She could use one to protect her from Gideon—or more accurately, to protect her from her own wayward nature.

To her surprise, he took her question seriously. "It might be wise, given their reaction yesterday."

"Come on, Gideon. You still haven't answered my question. What caused the fighting to break out?"

"Okay," he capitulated. "I'll tell you. It should serve as a good object lesson, if nothing else."

"Object lesson?" She wrinkled her nose. "I'm not going to like this, am I?"

"I doubt it." He cornered her near his desk. "I was able to acquire all three companies so easily for one simple reason."

She surrendered to the inevitable, accepting his proximity with a faint sigh that more likely had its origins in sheer pleasure than anything remotely attributable to professional regard. "And what was this one simple reason?"

"They were feuding among themselves and not paying attention to the bottom line. Their battle for domination gained more importance than their businesses. It became more vital than their families, their employees, even their own jobs."

She stared in dismay. It must have been a harsh lesson for the company heads involved. No doubt they'd deserved the reminder. But knowing Gideon, he'd have dished it out without hesitation, compassion or gentleness. "So you brought them all together to make that point."

"After which fingers were pointed, fists were thrown—"

"Dessert tables were set on fire."

A brief smile slashed across his face, bearing only the faintest resemblance to the endearing grin she'd known so intimately. The man she remembered was fading with frightening speed. If she hoped to find him again, she'd have to act fast.

Gideon inclined his head. "Worst of all, I lost most of my cache of scotch, half of which ended up on the walls and carpet."

"A tragedy," she murmured.

"If you'd tasted that scotch, you'd know how much of a tragedy."

"I gather you want me to explain the facts of life to the owners of these three companies a second time?"

"Yes. You can get the necessary names and numbers from my secretary, Lindsey. It shouldn't be difficult to arrange another meeting since they'll be feeling magnanimous, believing all is well with their tiny worlds. After that you're to tell them you're very sorry, but you made a mistake."

"Got it." She lifted an eyebrow. "As a point of interest, I assume I should duck around about then?"

He grimaced. "Either that or hide all the breakables. Particularly the scotch."

"No problem." She gathered up her purse and camera bag. "Leave everything to me."

She must have sounded a bit too accommodating, because he stilled, a ruthless quality entering his voice. "Don't screw this up, Piper. You *will* regret it."

No, *he'd* regret it if she didn't follow her instincts. But maybe she wouldn't explain that to him yet. Somehow she doubted he'd appreciate it. She flashed him a quick, reassuring smile as she headed for his office doors. Interesting. Suddenly she could breathe again. "Trust me, Gideon. I know what I'm doing."

"Why am I having so much trouble believing that?"

Definitely time to leave. "I can't imagine," she retorted. With an airy wave, she beat a hasty retreat before he realized his suspicions were correct—her agenda differed drastically from his own.

"All done?" Gideon asked.

"Everything's been taken care of," Piper assured, shoving the doors closed behind her. "Good grief, these things are heavy. I know you want to impress people, Gideon, but really. Think of your poor secretary, if nothing else."

"She says it takes the place of weight training."

Something in the way he made his comment kept her from laughing. She turned around, attempting to find him in the gloom of the office. His voice, a very exhausted sounding rumble, emerged from a collection of chairs and a sofa near the windows overlooking the city. A soft amber glow emanating from the Denver skyline provided the only illumination in the room. She fumbled her way to the sitting area and found Gideon reclining on the sofa, nursing a scotch.

"I see the rug didn't drink all your precious cache," she observed.

"Not now, pipsqueak." Ice rattled in his glass as he took a sip. "I don't have the energy to fight. If you'll save it for tomorrow, I'll be happy to accommodate."

She curled up in the chair closest to him. Something was wrong. Unfortunately she couldn't begin to guess what it might be. There had been a time when they'd been able to discern each others most intimate thoughts. But those days were long gone and this was a man she no longer knew nor understood. "Problem?" she questioned gently.

"Too many to count. And before you ask, I don't intend to discuss any of them with you."

"Because you're afraid I'll learn too much about you if you open up?"

His quiet laugh nearly broke her heart, the sound rife with pain. "Because it's none of your business. It hasn't been for five years, remember?"

It took her three tries to get the words out. "There isn't a day that's gone by that I haven't remembered," she admitted unevenly.

"Tell me about your meetings."

She didn't fight the change in topic. It was ironic that they both were experiencing similar emotions—a keen sense of loss and the torment that accompanied that loss—and yet didn't dare share their feelings. The danger of doing so was too great. A smoldering desire lingered despite all that had torn them apart, threatening to reignite with one careless word.

"I think the meetings went well." Popping the lens cover off her Leica Rangefinder, she adjusted the settings with practiced ease. "I'm going to take a picture of you now."

"I'd rather you didn't."

"I'm sorry, Gideon," she offered. "But I have to. It's sort of an obsession."

"I know all about obsessions." The comment was little more than a whisper. "I have a few of my own."

A strobelike flash lit the room and she caught a brief view of him. He was stretched out on the couch, one knee bent, an arm tucked behind his head, his bare feet sinking into the leather cushions. Dark hair fell across his brow in rumpled waves, uncovering the rebel beneath the businessman's guise. He wasn't wearing his suit anymore, not even a shirt. Instead he was dressed in well-worn jeans that molded to his hard masculine lines. There was a primitive grace in the way he relaxed that warned of a man not entirely at ease. Tension rippled beneath the surface, reminding her of an animal gathering itself in response to the first whiff of approaching danger, ready to attack at the least provocation.

This was the Gideon she knew and remembered, equal parts casual charmer and wary predator, switching from one to the other with breathtaking speed. Both had been learned responses to his early environment. He'd taught himself to use charm in an effort to become one with the people of Mill Run. But his visceral reaction to threat was a casualty of a childhood fraught with a brutality she could only imagine. With her, he'd lost that wild, defensive edge. He'd let down his guard and opened up.

He'd been the boy who'd taught her how to fish in the river by the old mill and helped her tear the ridiculous mounds of lace off her dresses so she didn't look so prissy. He was the teenager who'd taught her to throw and catch a baseball as well as any boy, and slide into first base without breaking her ankle. He'd also been the only one able to console her when she'd lost her mother to cancer. He'd held her in his arms with a compassion unusual in one so young and allowed her to soak an endless supply of shirts until over the months, her grief had gradually abated. And he'd been the man who'd loosened two of Freddie Collington's teeth when the football jock had decided taking her to the senior prom entitled him to shove his tongue in her mouth against her will while tearing at the most beautiful dress she'd ever owned.

Afterward, when her fear had turned to fury, Gideon had tossed her over his shoulder and carted her off so she wouldn't loosen a few more of Freddie's teeth. Then he'd helped repair her dress and taught her everything she'd ever needed to know about kissing. Real kissing. The kind that had ripped her world apart before setting it right again. He'd been her defender, her friend, her companion, as well as her fiercest supporter. Ultimately he'd become her lover, and she'd thought…her soul mate.

"Gideon," she whispered, aching at the slew of memories. It had been forever since she'd allowed herself to remember.

"Don't, Piper. We can't go there. It's too late for us."

She knew he was right. But there were so many questions that had gone unanswered for so long. Considering all she'd suffered at his hands, didn't she deserve an explanation? She'd come to terms with his callousness, dealt with it in her own fashion and eventually recovered. But handling the emotional fallout from those earlier events didn't stop her from wanting to know the reasons behind his actions. Especially when the "whys" had plagued her for all these years.

"What happened?" she demanded. "Can't you tell me that much?"

"You know what happened." He drained his glass

and reached out toward the table nearest to him. The tumbler clattered against the wooden surface. "Spencer happened. He stole the only two things I could claim as mine."

"He didn't steal anything—"

"Stop defending him!" Gideon erupted from the couch. For an instant she thought he'd yank her out of the chair and into his arms. At the last minute he veered toward the windows. Leaning his forearm against the double-glass pane, he gazed out at the city. "You always think the best of people, pipsqueak. But they don't always behave the way you expect. Sometimes they act totally out of character."

Was that all the explanation she'd get? Her jaw firmed. No. She wouldn't accept it. "Are you acting out of character now?"

"Yes."

The word was practically torn from him and Piper left the safety of her chair and approached. It was a risky move, but one she had to take. Every feminine instinct she possessed urged her to explore the broad expanse of his back, while every ounce of reason warned her against such a dangerous action. "How are you acting out of character, Gideon?"

"I'm hesitating. I have the opportunity to take down your brother and *dammit*!" His fist battered the heavy glass. "I'm hesitating like I did all those years ago."

She frowned in confusion. "I don't understand. How did you hesitate then?"

"I let Spencer get away with his accusations." His shoulders bowed, tension rippling across his back and shoulders, cording the powerful muscles. Her fingers itched to smooth away the knots of stress. Or was she simply longing to feel the warmth of his flesh beneath her hands? "I should have taken him down instead of letting him get away with what he did to me."

She stared in disbelief. How could he even suggest such a thing? A fury every bit as turbulent as his own gripped her. "You're wrong! That fight had a bad enough end without your making it any worse."

"*No!* I should have made certain Spencer ate every last accusation." Gideon spun around, his hands dropped to her shoulders. Despite the fierceness of his words and expression, his touch revealed a gentleness he'd have denied possessing. "Your brother stole my reputation. Hell, Piper, he shredded it. You were there. You know there was nothing I could do to defend myself against his accusations."

"He thought you'd burned the mill. He was mistaken. I did everything I could to make him see that, but—"

He cut her off without hesitation. "My word of honor was all I had. I came from a family of drunks and liars while having the misfortune of growing up in a small town with a long memory. You know I was a marked man from the day I was born. It took my entire life to prove that my word meant something. I didn't have money. I didn't have family connections. I didn't have any outside support. All I had to rely on was myself and the integrity I'd built over the years."

Piper's anger drained away, empathy allowing her to excuse his obsessiveness, even when every word reopened a wound she'd thought safe from harm. Her mouth twisted as she faced the unpalatable truth. She was a fool to still care, but that didn't change the facts. The depth of passion she felt toward Gideon remained, whether she wanted to feel that way or not. Otherwise, she'd never have returned, never have put herself in the line of fire.

Fortunately she'd forgiven him for the harm he'd done her, learned to deal with the injuries she'd suffered and moved on with her life. Apparently Gideon had been unable to do the same, which meant she had to find a way to prevent him from adding to the pain he'd already caused. She refused to allow him to dedicate his life to revenge. He deserved better. And so did Spencer.

"I know how difficult it was for you to overcome your background," she attempted to soothe. "And I admired the way you handled it. You were the most honorable man I'd ever known."

"Until your brother accused me of burning down his inheritance. From that moment on, my word didn't mean squat. The respect I'd spent years earning vanished. In the space of five short minutes I went from being a man of honor to one of those shiftless Harts who'd lie as soon as look at you."

"No, Gideon. There were some who believed in your innocence."

"You're wrong, Piper. They'd been waiting for me to prove I was no different than the rest of my family. It just took me longer to show my true colors."

He was killing her bit by bit. "Don't do this. You're eating yourself up inside over a mistake. You're allowing it to ruin your life."

His hands slid from her shoulders upward, sweeping along the sensitive expanse of her neck before sinking into her hair. "Maybe I could have handled it if Spencer hadn't also taken away something of even more value."

She stared in bewilderment. "More important than

your reputation? There wasn't anything more important.''

''There was you.''

That one simple statement provoked tears. ''No. Oh, no.''

''You sided with him, Piper.'' A bleak darkness emptied the spirit from his eyes. ''You claimed to love me. But you didn't. You couldn't. I sent you a note asking you to leave town with me, to start over. Have you any idea how long I waited for you? What I risked to take you with me?''

I sent you a note… I waited for you… It hurt to draw breath. He didn't know. Dear heaven above, he didn't know. That hadn't even occurred to her. All these years she'd thought he simply didn't care and instead, he'd never been told. ''Oh, Gideon,'' she whispered. ''You don't understand.''

''Understand what?''

She shook her head. ''I need time to think this through.''

His hands tightened in her hair and he tipped her face to his. She couldn't evade his ruthless gaze any more than she could escape the fierce determination she read there. ''Understand *what*, Piper?''

CHAPTER FOUR

PIPER refused to answer, despite the gathering frustration darkening Gideon's eyes. She needed information first. "What note? What note are you talking about?"

His frustration turned to anger. "The one I gave Jasmine for you. She swears she delivered it, so don't try to convince me she didn't. It won't work."

Piper could vaguely recall his youngest sister, a pint-size black-haired savage who'd run wild through the neighborhood, regarding all who approached with acute distrust and a distressing hint of fear. It was possible that Jasmine gave her a note. Her memory of that time was vague, at best. She moistened her lips, seeing a possible way out of their dilemma. "If...if I wasn't in any position to answer your note, would it make a difference?"

"To my plans for Spencer?"

"Yes."

He shook his head, urging her closer. Their bodies fit so well together, it made the emotional distance between them that much worse. "It wouldn't make the least difference. Your brother destroyed everything I'd built in Mill Run. Years of backbreaking work, gone with one unsubstantiated accusation. This isn't between you and me anymore, sweetheart. It's gone way beyond that." His hands still cupped her head. Once upon a time, it would have been a lover's embrace. But not any longer. There wasn't anything the least loverlike about his hold. "Now tell me what I don't understand about the day of the fight. Tell me something that I can give a damn about.''

It hurt. It hurt so much to have the answers he craved but be unable to give them to him. She couldn't tell him the truth, not in his current mood. She didn't dare. It would destroy something precious between them, a final link that still existed despite his denials. Perhaps after they'd had time to work together, after she'd had an opportunity to slip beyond the pain and bitterness, she could make him realize how that day had seen the ruin of them all.

In the meantime, she had to act before he forced an answer from her. Slipping her fingers into his hair in an exact imitation of his hold on her, she tugged his head down and with a gentling murmur, covered his mouth with hers. She could tell she'd taken him by surprise. Tension swept through his body, and for an instant she thought he'd reject her kiss. Then with a rough groan, he relaxed into it.

The unexpected joining was exquisite, every bit as good as it had been in the boardroom. Better. There he'd taken her by surprise and she'd acquiesced. But this time she was the aggressor. A resolve to enjoy her own impetuosity seized hold. The effect was mind-blowing. With one simple kiss, she tumbled into emotions she'd almost forgotten existed.

She molded her mouth over his, the damp heat causing a rumble to vibrate deep in his chest. Her lips parted and she invaded his mouth, staking a claim with delicious insistence. She'd never been shy about expressing her feelings. With Gideon, it had been pointless. He had a knack for uncovering her most closely held secrets.

She could only hope that wasn't still the case since

she desperately needed time—time to decide how to answer his demand, time to unravel the problems of their
past in slow, careful increments, time to find and reawaken the man she'd once known. Unfortunately Gideon
had never been the most patient of men, even under the
best of circumstances. And these were far from the best.

"You can't avoid my questions this way," he warned
in a voice husky with desire.

"Maybe not." She offered a teasing smile. "But at
least it's distracting you long enough to give me a few
minutes to think."

"In that case, take all the time you want." Determination gleamed, mingling with the desire. "I'll still get
my answers, no matter what it takes."

It made for an effective warning, though one she
couldn't bring herself to heed right now. She'd offered
the kiss as an excuse to avoid his question. But in reality,
it had exposed a very real craving. Unable to help herself, she bridged the distance between them and sealed
his mouth with hers once again.

The years they'd been apart had given her the opportunity for comparison. There had been other men in her
life, men she'd fooled herself into thinking she could
love. But something had kept her from making the ultimate commitment, preventing her from indulging in
any sort of serious or long-term relationship. Now she
understood why.

Their kisses had never made her lose all self-control.
Nor had they caused such a depth of desire that she'd
have allowed those others the latitude she granted
Gideon. Deep down, in the darkest recesses where brutal
honesty prevailed, she knew that if this particular man
chose to strip away her clothes and settle her onto the

carpet, she'd open herself and welcome him without hesitation or question. She wanted him that badly. Wanted
him, despite all that stood between them.

As though he sensed how she felt, he thumbed apart
the buttons of her blouse. It gaped and their breathing
grew labored, the very air thickening from the urgency
of their desire. For an instant time froze, while past and
present merged. The Gideon who'd been such a vital part
of her heart and soul stared through the eyes of the
Gideon who had allowed darkness to consume him—a
man who desperately needed her, whether he recognized
that need or not. It was a moment of choice and they
both knew it. She could either snatch her blouse closed
and walk away. Or she could follow her heart and step
into his arms. Perhaps if the room had been filled with
pitiless light instead of wrapped in protective shadows,
she wouldn't have had the nerve to go any further.

But insanity prevailed and she took that final step.

Her blouse dropped to the floor. Next the zip of her
skirt gave way, the rose-colored silk puddling at her feet.
He backed her toward the sofa, easing her downward.
He still wore his jeans, not that they'd last long.
Considering his state of arousal, they couldn't be terribly
comfortable.

Piper fought for sanity. It wasn't an easy proposition.
His flesh was hot beneath her fingertips, the muscles
across his back and shoulders rippling with every strok-
ing caress. He groaned, snatching a series of swift, potent kisses. And in between, his hands were everywhere,
working the clasp of her bra, following the indent of her
waist to the scrap of lacy silk clinging with stubborn
tenacity to her hips. She stiffened in his arms, aware that

not even the darkness of the room would keep her secret safe much longer.

"I didn't mean to distract you quite this well," she managed to say. The words ended in a soft gasp as his mouth closed over an erect nipple. "We're going to regret this tomorrow. You realize that, don't you?"

"Tough. I want you. Just this one last time."

Did he really mean that? "For old time's sake?" she asked painfully.

"This one night is all I'll need, I swear. After that, we can keep it as impersonal as you'd like."

A single night wasn't all she'd need. And she couldn't believe it would be enough for him, either, despite what he claimed. "After this you'll be satisfied?" She allowed herself a few precious seconds to reacquaint herself with the width of his shoulders and powerful contours of his chest. She knew this man, remembered each taut plane and hard curve. Heaven help her, how had she survived this long without him? And how could she ever let him go again? "We can forget this ever happened?"

"Not forget. Just—"

"Just not let it interfere with the rest of our business?"

He stopped the question with an impassioned kiss. "This has nothing to do with business."

"What does it have to do with?"

He exhaled sharply, the warmth of his breath bathing her bare shoulders. "Now you want to talk?"

"Before talking struck me as the more dangerous option." She fought to string words together, horrified to discover that reason was rapidly slipping away. "I've changed my mind about that."

"Maybe I can help you reconsider."

He levered upward, allowing a wave of cool air to wash away the scorching heat they'd generated. It afforded her a fleeting moment of sanity, one that vanished the instant he cupped her thighs. He parted them, his thumbs drawing lazy circles across the sensitive skin. Resistance didn't even occur to her, not even when he settled into the juncture. Only his gaping jeans and a thin layer of lace separated them. The rest was sheer heat.

"Do you remember?" he whispered. "Do you remember how it was?"

She shuddered. "How could I forget?" They'd shared warm summer nights, silvered in moonlight and sweetened by endless hours of lovemaking. The river would gurgle at their feet and the mill would creak on the hill while the night serenaded them with the unique music of Colorado's nightlife. Nothing could keep them apart back then. Life offered endless possibilities because they were together and in love. "Do you miss it?" she dared to ask.

"Some days." The door he'd barred against her cracked open, allowing her a brief glimpse of that long-ago man and the anguish he couldn't quite hide. "Some days it's a hunger that won't be sated, a favorite song I can't drown out. A longing. A regret. An ache that nothing can ease."

She held him close, wishing she could give him the solace he so desperately needed. "Then why, Gideon? If what we had meant so much, why can't we work out our differences?"

She could feel the tension return, feel him gathering himself, sense his rejecting her attempts to push past his barriers. "We're not going there, pipsqueak. I'm making love to you. Justify it any way that makes it acceptable. Whether it's for old time's sake, or because we never had the opportunity to say goodbye all those years ago, or because it's been too long since you were with a man. Personally I don't give a damn what excuse you choose. But this is sex, pure and simple. Don't try to pretty it up or give it any special significance. Got it?''

''Gideon, please.''

''You want me, Piper. You know you do.'' His arms tightened around her. The brush of skin against naked skin whispered an irresistible mating call. ''It's been too long for us. We need this. Badly.''

She couldn't deny it. ''I know, I know.''

''Then let it happen. You know it's what you want. It's what we've both wanted since you first walked in the door.''

''And afterward?''

''Dammit, Piper. Stop putting Spencer between us. Nothing's going to change my mind about him. Not even this.''

It hurt to keep talking, hurt to think, hurt to know that all Gideon needed from her was a quick, sordid coupling. She closed her eyes. She was an idiot to think it was more, that it might involve the heart. This had to do with a different part of his anatomy, altogether. ''Gideon, we can't do this. Not now. Not until we've had the chance to discuss the situation.''

''I'm only in the mood for one thing, and it sure as hell isn't a discussion.''

She could have wept with the desperation of her want. ''Okay, then answer one quick question.''

His mouth trailed from jawline to shoulder blade, before dipping lower. ''Fast. Ask me fast.''

She went with the first thought to pop into her head, one she prayed would distract him long enough for her to find where she'd misplaced her common sense. "Whose sofa is this?"

"*What?*"

"The sofa… It's a trophy, isn't it? Who did you take it from?"

The word he used brought bright color to her cheeks. "Not that again."

"We're making love on top of ruins, aren't we? Tell me whose. Did he want to be taken down? Does he mind that you have his sofa? Was it special to him the way the stirrup vessel was special to Archibald Fenzer?"

"Stop it, Piper."

"Does the pain of others matter so little to you anymore?"

He lifted upward again. This time the cold air that swept between them remained. "You've made your point. You've also managed to kill the moment. But then, I'm assuming that was your plan."

"I'm sorry, Gideon," she said with utter sincerity. "It was the only thing I could think of to stop you."

He escaped the couch. Crossing his office, he picked up her discarded blouse and skirt and tossed them to her. She didn't waste time looking for her bra. Dressing with impressive speed, she took a deep, steadying breath before turning to face Gideon once again.

"We have a lot of issues to deal with," she announced. To her relief her voice didn't betray the tumult of emotions rioting through her. "Not the least of which is what just happened on that couch."

He flicked a switch and stark light engulfed the room, burning a path over every surface and stabbing into every corner. It left Piper painfully exposed, which was undoubtedly his intention. She glanced around, thrusting a hand through her hair. What the *hell* had she done with her bra—or her shoes, for that matter? Maybe if she were fully dressed, she wouldn't feel so vulnerable.

Gideon approached, his expression as remote as she'd ever seen it. ''For your information, nothing happened on the couch. Nothing of significance, that is.'' The ruthless businessman had returned with a vengeance. Whatever doors he'd opened—doors that had briefly allowed her access to his inner sanctum—had been slammed shut, locked, barred and sealed against her. ''And the only issue we have to deal with is the manner in which you plan to fulfil the terms of Spencer's contract.''

''You're wrong, Gideon.'' How did she explain all her concerns, especially when he would neither acknowledge nor recognize their validity? ''You've changed.''

''Let me guess…'' His mouth twisted. ''It's not for the better.''

''Not when all your actions are focused on either revenge or—'' She gestured to indicate their surroundings. ''Or on deconstructing everything you come into contact with. Including me.''

''That's none of your business.''

She met his gaze unflinchingly. ''I'm making it my business. The Gideon I once knew can't be gone. If it's the last thing I do, I'm going to find him again. Or reawaken him.''

A rough laugh broke from him. ''You're joking.''

''Not even a little.''

''You think this is some sort of Sleeping Beauty

story? Only this time it's Prince Charming who's fallen under an evil spell?''

''Something like that.''

He leaned a hip against his desk and folded his arms across his chest. Without a shirt he looked dangerously masculine, the impression intensified by his gaping jeans. There had always been an animal wariness about Gideon, a raw, dangerous quality, as though he anticipated trouble around each and every corner. She had the distinct impression his current occupation intensified that aspect of his personality, honed the edges over the years they'd been apart rather than blunting them. She caught her lower lip between her teeth. What in the world had made her think she could tame such a determined predator? Optimism was one thing, but this…

Tilting his head to one side Gideon studied her with cold dispassion. ''What the hell makes you think I want to change?''

All right, so maybe she'd been foolish to think her kiss would reawaken the man she'd once known. And maybe her optimism was downright foolhardy. But she wouldn't give up on him. *She couldn't.* ''Your need for revenge has consumed you,'' she argued. ''If you keep going the way you are, there's no turning back. It'll change you permanently.''

''So?''

Didn't he understand? ''You're not that sort of man. I know you're not. Deconstructing companies, taking trophies, seeking revenge…it's made you hard, Gideon. It's made you ruthless.''

He actually laughed. ''And that's a bad thing?''

''Stop it! You know it's not right.''

''That sort of arrogance is going to rebound on you.''

He left his desk and approached. Grasping her arm, he tugged her close once again. ''I've always been this sort of man. You're the only one in all of Mill Run who never realized that. You stuck me on top of a white horse, garbed me in shiny armor and called me a knight. But that didn't make it true.''

Breathing became a struggle. Every sense awoke to him, responded to him. More than anything she wanted to tumble back onto the couch and lose herself in his embrace. ''Honor was everything to you,'' she managed to protest.

''And truth, and justice and the American Way. Quaint, but naïve.'' His amusement hurt more than she thought possible. ''Honor wasn't everything to me. It was everything to *you*. It was a means to an end.''

''What end?'' The words were painful to utter.

''Getting you.''

For a split second she actually believed him. Believed in his heartlessness. Believed in the darkness shadowing his soul. Believed that he'd taken a path that didn't offer the possibility of a safe retreat. The crippling weight of doubt felt like an impossible burden.

''Gideon,'' she whispered.

''Give me Spencer and you never have to see me again.''

She shut her eyes and fought back a laugh. He'd said precisely the wrong thing. Even if the situation with Spencer hadn't arisen, they'd still be facing this particular confrontation. He just didn't know it. Fate had an ironic sense of humor. She leaned into him, oddly comforted by his closeness. He smelled safe. He felt safe. Even as he hit out with words, he held her with a gentleness she couldn't mistake. He was born to protect, no matter what he said or how hard he fought against his nature.

"So you've turned into a ruthless bastard and there's nothing I can do to change you. Is that it?"

"That's about the size of it. But you don't have to stay here and watch. Nor do you have to participate. Give me what I want and you can leave."

"I am what you want, Gideon."

Muscles rippled along his jaw and he shook his head in futile protest. "You were, once upon a time. But you tried to wake me with your kiss, remember? It didn't work."

"I guess some spells are harder to break than others," she murmured wistfully.

He laughed at that, the sound rusty from disuse. "This isn't a spell you can break, pipsqueak." He swept a lock of hair behind her ear. It was a familiar gesture, one that came with an unconscious tenderness that she doubted he even noticed. "Get out of the way. We had some good times, times I'd rather not spoil by hurting you."

"Too late."

"So you've said. But the hurt you felt all those years ago won't compare to what I could do to you now," he warned.

She fought against the bleakness of memories from years long past. It was a cold, black place she had no desire to revisit. How could anything be as horrible as that? She pulled back to look at him. "You have no idea how wrong you are."

A deadly resolve dropped over his face, settling into the harsh planes with the ease of long familiarity. "Don't challenge me. You'll lose every time. I'm going to get what I want one way or another."

"We'll see."

He released her. "You can't win, Piper. You don't have the money to support yourself while you work for me, and you won't have the spare time to earn what you'll need to stay alive. Starting tomorrow you'll begin deconstructing your very first company. Or you can end it all by backing off and letting me work out the details with your brother."

"Not a chance."

"How's Spencer going to react when he discovers you've been fighting his battles?"

"Not well," Piper admitted. She caught a glimpse of her high-heeled shoes near the couch and crossed to slip into them. For some odd reason the added inches boosted her morale. "But he'll understand once I explain."

"Somehow I don't see Spencer taking your interference very well."

"He won't take it any better than you have—not that he'll have any more choice than you do." She summoned a cheerful smile. "I guess you'll both have to learn to live with it."

"Or you'll have to learn to live with how we negotiate around you. Because the minute I get hold of Spencer that's what I plan to do."

Which didn't give her much time. Fortunately her brother was out of the way in California hoping to attract investors interested in both the mill, as well as the revival of the town. But he wouldn't stay there for long. Two, three weeks at most. If she hadn't found a way out of their predicament by then, Gideon might succeed in his plan for revenge. Spotting her bra draped over the arm of the couch, she snatched it up and stuffed it into her camera bag. One way or another she had to find the man she once knew and set him free—no matter what it took.

"Thanks for the warning, Gideon." Gathering her possessions she headed for the door. Once there, she turned. "Now let me give you a warning. I'm not going to give up on you. You're stuck with me, whether you like it or not. And there are going to be some changes around here. So prepare yourself."

As an exit line, it was pretty good. Piper released her breath in an exasperated sigh. At least it would have been, if Gideon hadn't had to help her open the double doors so she could sweep grandly through them. Oh, well. If nothing else, she left him with a smile on his face. That was worth something, right?

"So where are we going?" Piper demanded.

Gideon maneuvered his car through the traffic clogging the Denver streets and spared her a quick glance. It never ceased to amaze him how upbeat she remained, regardless of the circumstances. After their discussion the night before, he half expected a certain storminess in her attitude. Instead she was sunny bright in perky yellow, her eyes as blue and cloudless as a summer sky. He gritted his teeth. And all he could think about was getting that perky yellow peeled off her and doing whatever it took to cloud those eyes with passion.

Dammit all! His grip tightened on the steering wheel. He wouldn't allow her to keep distracting him this way. *Filing.* That was it. He'd send her to accounting as a filing clerk. Maybe then he'd stop picturing her spread across his couch with nothing but a bit of lace clinging to her hips. After that he'd get rid of the damn couch, too. Because it was clear he wouldn't get much work done with that as a reminder. And then, just to be on the safe side, he'd—

"Gideon? Did you hear me? Where are we going?"

He swore beneath his breath. And then he'd have his head examined to find out precisely what was wrong with him. He'd never had trouble focusing before. At least... Not until Piper showed up. "I want to take a look at a business that's vulnerable right now and see if there's anything worth salvaging."

She brightened at that. "Salvaging. Good."

"Salvaging...as in worth breaking up and reselling for a profit."

Her pleasure faded to a frown of annoyance. "You're going to deconstruct them?"

He shrugged. "Deconstruct, dismantle, dismember. Take your pick."

"How very negative of you, Gideon. I'd think you'd find that very tiring after a while. Don't you ever get the urge to build something?"

He shot her an amused glance. "On occasion. But if I wait long enough it usually passes."

"Oh, very funny." Waves of displeasure rolled off her and as much as he'd like to continue to find humor in her disapproval, his smile faded. Somehow she'd managed to prick his conscience. Strange. He could have sworn he didn't have one anymore. "What sort of company are you investigating?" she asked.

"They're a small ski resort near the town of Happy. They've been in business for a couple of generations, but in the last few years there's been serious competition from other, larger outfits surrounding them. They've been going downhill for a while."

"Happy... That's where the jewelers have their head-quarters, isn't it?"

"Yes."

"Are you going to look them over, as well?"

"I did that months ago. Why?"

"Just wondering."

Something in her tone made him suspicious. "Listen to me, Piper. Right now I'm attempting to purchase the Tyler's resort. If you do anything to interfere with the negotiations you'll regret it. Are we clear on that?"

"Very clear."

He'd come down too hard. Not that she let on. Her tone remained calm and professional. But the sudden appearance of her camera and the determined whir of the advancing film as she took a series of pictures warned that she wasn't feeling particularly equitable.

"What are you going to call these?" he asked wryly. "Heartless Hart Hits the Highway?"

"Cute. But I was thinking of calling them Devil Driving."

"Has a nice ring."

"I thought so."

He waited a minute before offering, "It's business, Piper."

"No, Gideon," she corrected. "It's people's lives. I can understand your need to take revenge against Spencer and me. But what did Ramsey do to you? Or Fenzer?"

Not this again. "Are you still obsessing over my office furniture?"

"Yes."

He was definitely getting rid of that couch—before someone told her how it had come into his possession.

"Don't. Those men went out of business without any help from me."

"But you could have given them a hand," she argued. "Helped them. Maybe it would have made the difference between their succeeding and their going bankrupt."

He shook his head, adamant. "And by offering that helping hand I could have gone down with them."

"Sometimes doing the right thing comes with risks."

There was something in her voice that warned she spoke from personal experience. Was she referring to acting as Spencer's collateral? He couldn't imagine what else it could be. It sure as hell couldn't have anything to do with the day the mill burned. No one had done right on that occasion.

"I understand what you're trying to do, pipsqueak," he offered gently. "But it's not going to work. I am what I am. Take it or leave it. But I'd rather you did leave than to wear yourself out battling against the inevitable."

"But that would be giving up on you." She gave his knee a reassuring pat and he almost drove off the road. "And I'm not ready to do that."

He was a total idiot. He should have thrown her out when she first showed up. Failing that, he should have stuck her in some obscure division of his company where he wouldn't see her on a daily basis. *Filing.* Definitely filing. He downshifted and darted around a tractor-trailer rig. Yeah, right. That would work. No doubt he'd end up spending half his day reacquainting himself with whatever forgettable corner she occupied. Better to have her close so he could keep an eye on her.

That way he could make sure she didn't cause any trouble.

As a rationalization it worked for all of two seconds. "There are some files on the back seat. Get them."

"Yes, sir."

Clearly the request contained a bite he hadn't intended and he deliberately altered his tone. "Do me a favor and read through them."

There. That was better. He'd gone from sounding like a rabid tiger to merely sounding like one who'd caught his paw in a trap. A vast improvement, if he did say so himself. He slanted her a quick glance to see if she appreciated the difference and got a face full of camera for his effort. How he'd managed to get through the rest of the drive without losing his cool again, Gideon couldn't say. Not that Piper appreciated his restraint.

After reading through the file, she snapped it closed and swiveled in her seat to glare at him. "A family?" she demanded in outrage. "You're going to deconstruct over four generations worth of blood, sweat and tears?"

He ground his teeth together. She literally vibrated with righteous indignation which left him with only one option—to react defensively. It was a perfectly natural response. It sure as hell didn't mean he was in the wrong. "I'm thinking about it, yes."

"How can you even consider such a thing? The Tylers are one of the founding families of Happy. They came across the country in covered wagons. They literally carved out a life for themselves from the very earth beneath their feet."

"They were miners. And they did pretty damned well for themselves for a while. Is it my fault they didn't put all that money to good use?"

"The charities they started up wasn't putting their money to good use?" She didn't give him time to do more than wince before continuing. "Even after the mine played out, they were creative enough to come up with a new plan. A ski resort was pretty darned innovative when they first thought of the idea."

He set his jaw at a stubborn angle. "And now their new plan isn't working. They're out of options. They just don't realize it, yet."

"I'm sure you'll take pains to explain it to them."

Aw, hell. She was going to drive him insane. No doubt that was her plan. So far, it was succeeding beautifully. "I won't be explaining anything to them until I see whether or not I want to buy their resort. It may not be worth as much as they owe the bank."

"And if it is?"

"Then I'll make an offer over dinner tonight."

"Tonight?"

He took in her calculating expression and shook his head. "Don't even think about it. You're not invited."

"Afraid of what I might do?"

He shrugged off the taunt. "Your interference wouldn't change a thing. It would just make the situation more difficult than it needs to be."

She didn't offer any further comment until they arrived at the resort. What he hadn't expected were the tears that burned in her eyes as she stood outside the rambling mountainside chalet. For some reason they affected him more than anything she'd said so far.

"It's beautiful," she murmured after an endless moment. "No wonder four generations of Tylers have chosen to make their home here. If I'd been born into this, I wouldn't want to leave, either."

Unable to help himself, he wrapped his arm around her shoulders and tugged her close. "It reminds you of your family's mill, doesn't it?"

Her chin quivered for an instant before she firmed it. "Our mill became obsolete the way the Tylers's resort has. Spence's idea to restore the mill as a tourist attraction was a good one, an idea that would have had a huge impact on the entire town. It's too bad these people can't do something similar."

"I don't see it happening. They don't have enough property to compete with the larger ski resorts in the area. But with serious renovations I bet this place could be turned into a winter home for some Hollywood types."

She nodded reluctantly. "Or someone who's gotten rich off tech stocks over the past few years and is looking to throw away a handful of his millions."

"Good idea."

She released her breath in a long, quavering sigh and it took every ounce of self-possession to keep from comforting her with a kiss. He hadn't lost all his marbles. Not yet, anyway. A single kiss and that pretty little dress of hers would go from perky yellow to grass-stained green. Deliberately he released her and returned to the car.

"So what now?" she asked.

He opened the passenger door for her. "Now we head back to Denver where I do some more research, crunch some numbers and come to a decision."

Her hands clenched at her sides. "And then?"

"And then I make the Tylers an offer they'd be wise not to refuse."

"Unless a better idea presents itself," she whispered.

Gideon grimaced. Now why did that sound like a warning? And why did he have a feeling she'd find a way to act on that warning? He shook his head. This was what he got for being such a damned pushover and letting Piper stay. Next time she tried to force him in a direction he didn't want to go, he'd put his foot down. He'd simply tell her no.

Oh, yeah. That would work.

CHAPTER FIVE

"BILL, I don't see that you have any other choice,"
Gideon explained patiently. "Either you sell out or you
face bankruptcy. At least by selling you can realize a
small financial gain."

"The bank—"

Gideon shook his head. "Sorry to break the news, but
the bank isn't going to help you. They want their money,
and they want it now. That leaves me as the only way
out of your predicament."

Bill's mouth tightened. "You're buying our note from
the bank, aren't you?"

"Yes."

"We've heard about you, Hart," Tyler's son cut in.
"And none of it's good."

Jarrett had all the passion of youth and none of the
ability to control it. No doubt age and a few hard knocks
would correct that oversight. Otherwise, the kid was in
for a rough time of it. Gideon could have described some
of the tougher lessons he'd swallowed during his years
in Mill Run, but it wouldn't do any good. Some lessons
had to be experienced firsthand.

"You've seen the bottom line," Gideon continued to
address the senior Tyler. "You can't make it through
another season. Your choices are limited."

Jarrett thrust his dinner plate toward the center of the
table. "What you mean is, if we don't sell, you'll force

us into bankruptcy. Well, let me tell you where you can shove—''

The peal of the doorbell drowned out the rest of Jarrett's comment. Not that there was much question about what he intended to say. It was an expression Gideon had heard before and would no doubt hear again in the years to come. He fought back an understanding smile, knowing it wouldn't be appreciated. ''Excuse me, won't you?'' he said pleasantly.

Considering his apartment was on the top floor of his office building, he didn't often have visitors drop by unannounced. For one thing, the security guards wouldn't let them through without calling first. Which meant there were only two possibilities. Either one of his sisters stood on his doorstep, or—

''Hello, Gideon. Give me a hand, will you?'' Piper breezed past. ''Could you grab some of my bags? The security guards were sweet enough to help me lug all this stuff up here, but they needed to go back to guarding and securing, or whatever it is you have them doing. I told them you and I could take it from here.''

''Take what from here?'' He poked his head into the hallway. A half-dozen suitcases, twice as many boxes and an odd assortment of plastic bags and paper sacks littered the area outside his living quarters. ''What the *hell's* going on, Piper?''

''Isn't it obvious? I'm moving in.'' She paused in the doorway leading to the dining room. ''Oh! I forgot you were planning to have company this evening.''

Gideon gritted his teeth. Piper Montgomery had to be the worst liar he'd ever met. ''You knew damn well—''

She ignored him and approached his guests with an outstretched hand. ''You must be Bill Tyler.'' Her greeting came with a natural warmth and openness that Gideon had always envied. "What a pleasure to meet you. I'm Piper Montgomery, by the way."

Bill studied her with acute suspicion before finally accepting her hand. "You're Hart's woman?"

She laughed in genuine amusement. "Goodness, no."

Next she offered her hand to Jarrett. He hesitated even longer than his father, regarding her with an animosity that was almost a physical presence. For an instant Gideon thought he'd be forced to defend Piper, a confrontation he'd prefer to avoid. Fortunately the kid thought better of saying anything unforgivably rude and took her hand in a quick, reluctant shake.

Turning to Bill, she offered her most brilliant smile. "I'm not Hart's woman. It's far worse than that, I'm afraid. I'm his collateral." She glanced over her shoulder at Gideon and lifted an eyebrow, pure mischief glittering in her gaze. "Have I phrased that right?"

He closed his eyes and swore.

"Oops. I guess not."

Tyler's suspicion turned to confusion. "Excuse me? Collateral?"

She perched on the chair closest to him, making herself at home. "That's right. Collateral on my brother's loan."

Tyler shook his head. "I'm sorry. I still don't understand."

"It's really quite simple. You see, Spence—that's my brother—borrowed money—not from Gideon, but that's another story—and he either has to pay it back or offer something of equal value. I'm the equal value." She eyed the dinner table with unmistakable greed. "I'm starving. Mind if I help myself to a few of those carrots?''

"Piper," Gideon managed to grit out a warning. Not that she listened. But then, why should tonight be different than any other occasion?

"You can't spare me a few measly carrots?" she demanded. Her outrage sounded almost convincing. At least it must have to the Tylers. Obviously sensing a sympathetic audience, she confided, "I haven't eaten dinner. Couldn't afford it, if you want the truth. Being collateral can be tough on the bank account."

Bill's gaze switched from Piper to Gideon and back again. "This is preposterous. How can you be collateral on a loan for your brother?"

Gideon gave up. Folding his arms across his chest, he leaned against the doorjamb and waited with fatalistic interest for Piper to finish destroying his business deal. "Yes, pipsqueak. Tell them what an unconscionable bastard I am. They'll believe it, I guarantee."

She shrugged. "Okay." Snatching a carrot from the bowl, she snapped off a bite. "To be perfectly honest, it was all my idea. I offered to be collateral."

Jarrett jerked upright. "*Offered?* To…to…give yourself to him, you mean?" He stared at her in horror. "Why would you agree to that?"

"Give myself?" She managed a delicate blush and Gideon shook his head in admiration. How the hell did women do that? It must be programmed in their genes. "Oh, no. You don't understand. I'm not *that* sort of collateral."

Jarrett's face reddened, as well. "Then what?"

She explored the contents of a nearby dish and came away with a handful of olives. "You see, my brother needs another year to get his mill up and running. That's what the money was for. To renovate his flour mill and some of the other turn-of-the-century shops and buildings on our property. He's going to turn them into a tourist attraction and save our town from financial disaster by bringing in outside dollars. Then he'll be able to pay off his debt to Gideon.''

Tyler appeared intrigued. ''Interesting idea.''

''I thought so, too. But when Gideon bought out the note—''

''Why does that sound familiar?'' Jarrett muttered.

''You, too?'' she asked sympathetically.

Tyler grimaced. ''It's beginning to look that way.''

''Anyway, Gideon wants his money now, instead of waiting another year. So I came up with a scheme that would allow Spence to keep the mill, while satisfying Gideon's demand.''

''Just for the record, I'm far from satisfied,'' he thought to mention.

She leaned in closer to the Tylers. ''That's because he's impossible to satisfy.'' She offered the observation in an undertone that carried clear across the room, and probably into the next one, as well.

''Not impossible.'' He fixed her with a stare that warned of future retribution. ''I have a few suggestions that would afford me full satisfaction.''

She clasped her hands to her breasts in such a dramatic gesture it should have had everyone in the room cracking up. But as far as Gideon could tell, no one's mouth so much as twitched. ''See what I mean?'' she said. ''How am I supposed to react when he makes a comment like that?''

''My dear, I don't know what to say.'' Bill frowned

in concern. "Surely, there's some other option available to you?"

Piper heaved a heartrending sigh. "It's only for a year. It won't be too bad," she claimed bravely. "Or it wouldn't if all my money weren't going toward paying back the loan. That's why I'm here. I don't have enough to live on. Either I move in with Gideon or I find a comfortable place to sleep on some deserted street corner."

Bill jerked as though touched by a live wire. *"My God!"*

She went back to snitching food from Gideon's plate, the very picture of the poor, starving waif. He'd have applauded if he thought he could get away with it without having his head handed to him. "I figured since he was taking all my money, he'd have to take me, too."

"I don't get it," Jarrett interrupted. "How can he take all your money unless you agree?"

She batted her big baby blues at him. "Didn't I mention?" she asked with all the innocence of a coiled rattlesnake. "I have to work for him until my brother's debt is paid off. He's my boss. He tells personnel to keep all my money...and they do."

Bill shot to his feet. "This is despicable, Hart. I'd heard rumors about you. But even I didn't suspect you were capable of this sort of depravity."

Gideon inclined his head. "That's me. Depraved to the core."

"It's a shame, you know." Piper filched another piece of chicken from his plate. "He used to be the sweetest man in the world."

"I think 'sweet' is a bit much, pipsqueak."

"Sweet," she maintained stubbornly. Pouring a glass

of wine, she offered it to Bill. "It's such a sad story. Why don't you sit down and I'll tell you all about it?"

Gideon stiffened. "Oh, no you won't."

Tyler took the glass of two hundred dollars a bottle wine and swallowed half of it in a single gulp. Then he plunked himself down beside her. "Yes, Hart. I believe she will. Have a seat, Jarrett. I want you to listen to this, too. See how a man starts himself on the wrong path in life."

"Great," Gideon muttered. "I've become an object lesson."

Tyler actually had the nerve to quiet him with a wave of his hand before settling his full attention on Piper. "Now tell me what happened. I'd like to know."

She poured herself a glass of wine, as well, and took an appreciative sip. "Great stuff you have here, Gideon."

"I'm delighted you approve. I'll be sure to pass on your compliments to the Rothschild estate."

Aside from a swiftly suppressed grin, she ignored his remark, keeping her focus centered on Tyler. "This occurred years ago, you understand, when Gideon wasn't much older than your son." Pulling Gideon's plate closer, she helped herself to more of his chicken. "He was accused of a terrible crime. Arson, to be precise."

"*Arson!*"

"He was innocent, of course," she hastened to reassure between bites. "But it completely destroyed his reputation."

"Destroyed him, huh?"

"After years and years of hard work."

"Oh, for crying out loud." Couldn't they see she was overdramatizing the entire event? "Piper—"

His interruption earned him a glare. "This is my story, Gideon. I'd like to tell it my way."

"Let the girl, speak," Tyler agreed. "No point in squabbling over minor details. If she says you were destroyed, who are you to argue?"

Gideon lifted an eyebrow. "I don't know," he offered dryly. "The one who actually lived through it?"

"Those personally involved aren't always the best judge of these situations," Piper argued.

Tyler nodded in approval. "Quite right."

Satisfied they were in accord, she topped off his glass. "Up until that point, Gideon had spent his youth taking care of his mother and sisters. All six of them. Can you imagine? Providing for them, working his fingers to the bone, doing everything he could think of to prove his worth." She paused in her recitation long enough to examine the broccoli decorating Gideon's plate. With a shrug, she dug into that, too, though with far less enthusiasm than she'd shown for his chicken. "And he didn't just take care of his family. Oh, no. If there was a wrong out there, Gideon was bound and determined to right it."

"This *is* Hart we're talking about?"

Her jaw shot out at the hint of sarcasm coloring Tyler's voice. "He was a veritable knight in shining armor, no matter what he claims to the contrary. I mean the whole package. Got it?" She ticked off on her fingers. "White knight. Shiny armor. Snorting horse. Pointy lance—no pun intended. And all the other stuff knights need in order to do their knighting."

"You forgot the lady fair," Gideon murmured.

To his dismay her mouth quivered. She snatched a quick, steadying breath and inclined her head in agreement. "And a lady fair. And then one day the people in the town where he grew up took it all away from him."

"Took?" Gideon straightened from his lounging position, fighting off a sudden flash of anger. "Hell, sweetheart. They ran me out of town. If you're going to tell the story, get the facts straight."

She swiveled to stare in disbelief, wine sloshing over the brim of her glass. "What?"

Her shock wasn't an act. Interesting. "Didn't anyone tell you?" he asked softly.

"Oh, Gideon." Tears glittered in her eyes. "Is *that* why you left? They made you go?"

"To be honest, I didn't feel much like arguing with the shotgun they shoved in my gut."

"Shotgun?" She carefully returned her wineglass to the table. "Are you saying they threatened you with *guns?*"

He shrugged. "Okay, fine. It was only a single gun. But the one they chose was impressive enough to persuade me to go along with their plan." He regarded her with a healthy dose of skepticism. "You really didn't know? The way gossip spreads in Mill Run?"

She thrust the plate away and curled deeper into the chair. This time her waiflike appearance looked uncomfortably real. "No one would talk to me about you. Anytime I'd ask, they'd change the subject."

Bill Tyler's expression filled with parental concern. "So you two knew each other back then? Childhood sweethearts?" he guessed.

Piper swiped at the tears clinging to her lashes and nodded. "I wish you'd met him in those days, Bill. You'd have been so impressed. He always lived by the motto that a man's word of honor meant everything. But that all changed after he was falsely accused. *He* changed. Now he doesn't trust anyone. And instead of helping people build their lives, he sees everything and everyone as a commodity to be bought or sold. Now isn't that sad?''

''Very.''

Piper smiled through her tears. ''I knew you'd think so.''

Gideon thrust a hand through his hair. ''I don't believe this,'' he muttered.

''It's the truth,'' she maintained with foolhardy loyalty.

She was wrong and he had to make her see that. He couldn't allow her to continue viewing him through the eyes of an adoring twenty-year-old. He wasn't that man, anymore, and hadn't been for a very long time. ''What happened in Mill Run is ancient history. It doesn't have anything to do with our current situation.''

She offered a blinding look of unwavering faith. ''Of course, it does.''

Gideon's hands folded into fists. Why? Why did he have to hurt her again? Why couldn't she see him for what he was and play it smart? Any other woman would have caught one glimpse and kept as far away from him as possible. But not Piper. For some reason she desperately needed to believe in him. If it was the last thing he did, that would end here and now. He was going to explain the hard, cold facts, whether she wanted them or not.

''Would you like to know how Hart & Associates got its start?'' he asked.

''You mean, how you decided to deconstruct companies for a living?'' She made herself more comfortable. ''I'd love to hear the story.''

Blunt. Brutal. And fast. He'd tell it and get them all the hell out of his apartment. No doubt they'd be only too eager to leave. Then he'd polish off the rest of the wine, and maybe open another bottle for good measure. All this warmth and compassion had put him in the mood to get stinking drunk. ''After I was tossed out of town, I went to work for a small consortium of crooks.''

Piper swept her hand through the air in a gesture of dismissal. ''You'll never convince me you knew they were crooks when you took the job.''

He shifted impatiently. ''Fine. I didn't know, but—''

''See?'' she murmured to Bill.

''Dammit, Piper! Even if I had known, I still would have gone to work for them. At that point, I really didn't give a damn. They offered me money and I was happy to do whatever they asked in order to earn it.''

''Because you had to support your mother and sisters, right?''

He gritted his teeth, refusing to confirm her guess. ''This consortium set me up. They were bilking their customers and planned to use me as the fall guy. Considering my reputation in Mill Run, it wouldn't have been difficult to convince law enforcement that I was the culprit.''

''What did you do when you found out about their plan?'' Jarrett demanded, clearly fascinated.

Aw, hell. How had he managed to win over the kid? That wasn't part of his plan. ''I turned the tables on them. I played them at their own game. I managed to get damning information on one of the partners.'' He shrugged. "There was a reward. And I took every last penny."

Piper grinned at the Tylers. "Didn't I tell you he was a sweetie?"

"Nice work, Hart," Bill said with an approving nod.

Why weren't they listening to him? What happened to his being a devious, depraved bastard? "I'm not finished. I took the reward money and went after the others involved."

Jarrett pumped the air with his fist. "Excellent!"

Son of a bitch. They still didn't get it. Did he have to spell it out in single syllable words? "I used every devious method at my disposal to make them vulnerable and then take them down," he bit out. "It didn't matter how dirty, it didn't matter whether my methods were on the shady side of the law, it didn't even matter if innocents got in the way. They were going to pay and I was the one who planned to collect."

Jarrett whistled in admiration. "Way to go. Wish I could have been there to see that."

The muscles in Gideon's jaw clenched so tight it was a wonder he could force any words out. "I. Took. Revenge. Don't you understand? That's a bad thing!"

"Yes, it was," Piper agreed. "And you shouldn't encourage him, Jarrett. All that anger and aggression put Gideon on the wrong path. Hasn't it, Bill?"

Comprehension dawned in the older man's eyes. "Of course. I should have seen it for myself." He glanced at Gideon and shook his head in dismay. "No wonder you regard everyone as the enemy. You've been fighting the bad guys for so long, you've forgotten how to deal with the good ones."

"The *hell* I have—"

Tyler actually had the nerve to make solicitous *tutting* noises. "Now don't you worry, son. We'll work with you on this. I'm sure Piper and I can help turn you around."

Piper nodded vehemently. "Absolutely."

"Havin' too much fun walking on the wild side, huh, Mr. Hart?" Jarrett chuckled. "I would, too, especially if it meant making those crooks pay for all the rotten things they'd done."

Gideon exploded. "Have the three of you lost your collective minds? I'm doing precisely what I want, how I want, and when I want. Dammit, I like what I do."

"But at least you've realized that it's not what you *should* be doing," Piper soothed. "Not to innocent folks like the Tylers."

Bill nodded sagely. "Suggests there's hope for you, my boy," he agreed. "It's a step in the right direction."

An odd noise escaped Gideon's throat, a low, grating sound somewhere between a growl and a groan. He fought desperately for control. It had taken him a while, but he'd finally begun to understand the problem. Why hadn't he seen it sooner? Piper had infected the Tylers with her own peculiar brand of insanity. It must be contagious. All she had to do was walk in a room and people lost every ounce of reason and intellectual ability. A strange calm settled over him.

"I think my first mistake was opening the door," he observed to no one in particular. "My second was not throwing her out the second she pushed her way in."

"You do right by this girl," Bill admonished. "It's clear she's been crazy about you for years now. Why, I'll bet she stood by you when no one else would."

"I tried." Regret dimmed Piper's eyes. "But I didn't succeed."

Bill patted her hand. "Couldn't have been easy to stand up for him when he'd taken off. Left you all on your own, defending him without a lick of outside help."

"I didn't leave," Gideon protested. "Haven't you been listening? I was *run off*."

"If I were as rich as you, Mr. Hart, I'd have gone back and made them listen," Jarrett said with youthful candor.

"I'm sure he'll come to that same conclusion, eventually. Come along, Jarrett. Time for us to go." Bill pushed back his chair and stood. Crossing the room, he clapped Gideon on the shoulder. "I think you and I can do business after all, once we've gotten you back on the right track. What do you say?"

"I can't even begin to think what to say to that," Gideon admitted with utter sincerity.

"A simple 'you're welcome' will do. You have real promise, my boy. Hang on to Piper this time around and you'll go far." Tyler lowered his voice. "At first I thought you were serious about this collateral nonsense. But now I see it's your way of keeping her close until you can straighten out your differences. Smart move, if you ask me. And how's this…? If you two want to honeymoon at my resort I'll put you up in our best suite, no charge."

"If that day ever comes, you won't have to put us up." If he could only punch something, Gideon reflected. It would really, truly help. "I'll own the resort."

Bill chuckled. *"Ri-i-ight."* He glanced at his son and jerked his head toward the door. "Let's go, Jarrett. We'll give Piper a chance to work out the details with Gideon.''

''Don't worry about a thing. I'll take it from here,'' she promised.

''And I look forward to a call when you've come up with a plan.''

''You've heard my plan,'' Gideon thought to mention.

Bill shook his head in amused exasperation. ''I've heard Plan A. I think I'll wait to hear Plan B before reaching any decisions.''

Enough was enough. ''There isn't a Plan B.''

''Maybe not yet.'' Bill grinned. ''But I suspect there will be by the time that gal of yours gets through with you.''

There wasn't much point in saying anything further. The instant the Tylers had left, Gideon turned to confront Piper. ''Let me guess,'' she said with one of her pathetic sighs. ''First thing tomorrow you want me to call Bill and explain the facts of life to him, too.''

''You've got that right.'' He stabbed a finger at the door, his tone one of utter disbelief. ''They were feeling sorry for me.''

She stirred in protest. ''Not sorry, exactly. But they were definitely sympathetic with all you've gone through.''

''Sympathetic? Sympathetic! Dammit, woman!'' he roared. ''They're supposed to be scared of me, not sympathetic.''

Her brows drew together. ''Gee...I don't know, Gideon. I don't think trying to scare them is going to work very well.''

His jaw came together with a snap and he shoved the words through gritted teeth. ''Not after you got through with them, no." He prodded one of her suitcases out of his path. "And what's with all this stuff?"

"I told you. I'm moving in."

"The hell you are."

"You're right. The hell I am. It's all your fault, anyway," she accused. "I wouldn't have to impose if you hadn't been so clever."

"Clever?" He fought to remain coherent. If he didn't know better, he'd swear there was actual steam gathering between his ears. "Sweetheart, if I were so all-fired clever you wouldn't be here, the Tylers would have signed on the dotted line by now and I wouldn't be ready to do serious mayhem to anyone within arm's length."

She took a hasty step backward. "What I mean is... How am I supposed to live without any money? If you want to keep it all, then you're going to have to deal with the consequences."

He glared at the suitcase at his feet. "And I assume those consequences are scattered all over my doorstep?"

"Most of them." She twisted her hands together, the knuckles bleaching a telltale white. "What you see here is pretty much all the possessions I have in the world."

He thrust a hand through his hair. Hell's bells and little fishies. What did she have to go and say that for? "I'm surprised you didn't use that line on Tyler," he muttered.

"I would have if I'd thought of it." She tilted her head to one side and attempted to produce a smile. "What do you think? Too over the top?"

Apparently not, considering the odd tightness that had fisted in his chest the minute he'd heard it. "You're probably the only woman I know who could get away with it," he admitted grudgingly.

Her smile grew, lighting up her face in the sort of teasing look no one else dared use with him. Not anymore. Until that moment, he hadn't realized how much he missed the camaraderie they'd once shared. It filled some deep, dark hole, feeding a need he wasn't even aware he still possessed.

"And you're probably the only man I know who'd let me get away with it," she responded, a hint of relief underscoring her words.

"You think I'm a pushover?"

She held up her hands in a defensive gesture. "Not at all. I just think your reputation for being rough and tough is exaggerated."

"Exaggerated?" She had to be joking. "If you're basing that impression on the fact that I've indulged you these past several days, I suggest you reconsider your conclusions."

"I don't need to reconsider. I know you, Gideon. You always confront the world with your fists up, expecting the worst. But that's a defense mechanism." She gazed at him with an expression that warned she truly believed what she was saying. "Underneath you're kind and considerate and warm and generous."

She'd managed to steal every scrap of humor from the situation. He didn't want her thinking the best of him or believing in the fairy tale she'd built around him. Calling him a knight wouldn't make it true, any more than describing him in such glowing terms would magically imbue him with those characteristics. He wanted her to see him as he was—the real Gideon—not the mythical man she'd created from quixotic wishes and longlost dreams.

His hands folded into fists. "It would seem I've given

you the wrong impression,'' he said with painstaking formality. ''Clearly I've been too easygoing.''

Her mouth dropped open. ''You call your actions to date easygoing?''

''Without question.'' He took a step closer. ''Trust me, you don't want to see me any other way. But you will if you keep pushing.''

''Sometimes pushing is the only way to get through to you.'' She glared in exasperation. ''Though now that I 'reconsider' the matter, dropping a brick on your head may be an even better plan.''

''You know…I'm finally beginning to understand,'' he said contemplatively. ''First you meddled in the contract with Spencer. Then came the business with the jewelers. And now there's this latest disaster with the Tylers. I think I see where I've gone wrong.''

''Great. I knew you'd eventually realize your mistakes.'' She closed the final step separating them. Planting her hands on her hips, she shoved her nose to within inches of his. ''Now all you have to do is correct them. Tell everyone you've changed your mind. Tell them you've decided to start constructing instead of tearing things apart and everything will be fine.''

He continued as though she hadn't spoken. ''I've let you have your way each occasion we've locked horns and you've come to the logical, if erroneous, conclusion that I'll agree to all of your demands. I'll have to figure out what I can do to correct that.'' He jerked his head in the direction of her suitcases. ''Starting with this latest stunt.''

''It's not a stunt,'' she instantly denied.

''You can't seriously expect to move in here?''

''Hel-lo? Weren't you standing here when I explained

this earlier? Or was that a different Gideon Hart? Maybe one who actually has a heart.'' She counted off on her fingers. ''No money, no apartment, no food. I guess that means that, yes. I seriously expect to move in here.''

''Spencer—''

''Lives in Mill Run. Moving in with him would make the commute a bit lengthy. Wouldn't you agree?''

''Dammit, Piper.'' His frustration mounted, but other than flinging her out on the streets, he didn't see how he could reasonably get rid of her. ''This isn't my problem.''

''Maybe not, but it's a problem of your creation.''

The woman was being deliberately obtuse. ''That was the whole point. You were supposed to be left with no alternative other than to move aside while Spencer and I sorted out our differences.''

Her eyebrows shot up at that. ''Sorted them out? Cute. You mean, I was supposed to move aside while you took my brother apart piece by piece.''

''If it makes you happy to hear me admit it, okay, fine. That's what I meant.''

She smiled sweetly. ''Too bad. You started this and I'm dumping the situation back on your doorstep where it belongs. Literally. It's about time you learn that actions have consequences.''

Now she'd gone and made him really mad. ''Is that so? Honey, keep yankin' my chain and you're gonna get a snoot full of consequences.''

Aside from a little extra color washing across her cheekbones, she didn't respond to his threat. ''Will you help me drag this stuff in here or do I have to do it by myself?'' she demanded instead.

''Why the hell should I help? I don't have to put up

with this, you know.'' Yeah, right. Keep telling yourself that, buddy boy. ''All I need is one good excuse for throwing you out—just one—and you're gone.''

She waved that aside. ''I'm sure I'll give you dozens.''

He thrust his index finger in the air and shook it in her face. *''Just. One.''*

Her eyes flashed dangerously. ''One? Great. How about this... I'm going to bed.'' She bent over and heaved her suitcase into her arms. ''I'll leave you to lug the rest of my stuff in all by your lonesome.''

''The hell I will!''

''You can kick them around instead of me, if it makes you feel better. But watch the boxes. They're full of my photographs. Harm one picture.'' She grappled with her suitcase so she could thrust her own finger in the air— not her index finger—and shook it in his face. *''Just. One.* And there will be more than hell to pay.''

With that, Piper stalked deeper into his apartment. Unfortunately she'd forgotten one minor detail. Stopping dead in her tracks, she glanced over her shoulder with a chagrined expression. ''Normally I'd go to my room and punctuate all that by closing the door just shy of a slam.''

Gideon released his breath in a long sigh. ''Down the hallway. Second door on the right.''

''Thanks.'' She cleared her throat. ''I'm still mad at you, you know.''

''I didn't doubt it for a second.''

''Okay. I just wanted to make that clear. Good night, Gideon. Thank you for putting me up.''

''Night, pipsqueak. And you're welcome.''

CHAPTER SIX

PIPER crept from her bedroom and down the hall toward the entranceway of the apartment. Sleep had proved elusive, her insomnia either the result of her recent argument or—more likely—knowing Gideon slept mere feet away. Whatever the cause, she'd needed to get to her photographs. For some reason they managed to relax her, perhaps because they kept her grounded. In her experience, photos didn't lie—at least, not the ones she took. Even when they portrayed an unpalatable truth, at least it was a truth she could trust.

To her surprise, Gideon had brought all her bits and pieces inside the apartment. Well, what had she expected? For him to leave everything scattered across his doorstep? He'd never act in such a callous manner, no matter how much he thought he'd changed over the past several years. She frowned. It bothered her that he considered himself so hard and merciless. Perhaps that explained why he made so many uncharitable business decisions. He needed to prove the accuracy of his own self-image. And perhaps that's what had drawn her to the photographs.

She needed to prove him wrong.

The boxes had been neatly stacked in Gideon's study, next to his desk. It was a far different desk than the one he occupied downstairs in his office and, at a guess, he used it for personal business. Instead of a huge shiny black expanse that crouched on his carpet like a deadly spider, this one was a soothing golden brown fashioned from sturdy, old-fashioned oak. Interesting. It was as though the two desks mirrored the disparate sides of his personality. The surface was barren of papers and she took advantage of that fact to deposit one of her boxes on top before switching on the desk lamp. And that's when she saw him.

"Gideon!" He was stretched out on the couch in a position almost identical to the one she'd found him in after her meeting with the jewelers. And like that other occasion, he wore a pair of faded jeans and little else. "I didn't realize you were in here. Couldn't you sleep, either?"

"No."

"Because of your meeting with the Tylers?" she asked, hoping against hope he'd confirm her guess.

"No, not them."

She snapped her fingers, taking another wild stab. "I know. It's because you've decided to see if your armor still fits before you mount your white horse again and go charging into battle. But since it's been so long, you've forgotten how." She offered an encouraging smile. "Am I right?"

"Not even close."

Too bad. Still... A damsel-in-distress could hope. She shot him a quick glance. With luck, he'd reject her next guess, as well. "Is it because I'm here?"

"Bingo." He stirred, the leather cushions creaking beneath his weight like a well-used saddle. "What *are* you doing here, if you don't mind my asking?"

"Thought I'd go through some of my photos."

"Looking for anything specific?"

Yes. "No."

He clearly didn't believe her, but he let her get away with the small lie. "If all you're after is killing some time, explain something to me, Piper."

"If I can." She'd have been happier continuing their discussion if she weren't doing it in a thin cotton nightshirt. But then, he'd seen her in far less. And though he stared at her with a certain earthy interest, he didn't appear ready to pounce and have his wicked way with her. A shame, really. A man hadn't had his wicked way with her in the true sense of the word since... Well, since Gideon. She put that thought firmly out of her head before it got her into trouble. "What do you want explained?" she asked.

"Your photographs are magnificent. Why shove them out of sight in a bunch of boxes?"

"Oh, that." She shrugged. "These are duplicate prints I like to go through on a regular basis, so I keep them close by. The actual negatives and proofs are at my studio."

She'd surprised him. "Your studio?"

"That's where I take my wedding portraits. And before you try to question the expense," she added defensively, "the lease is prepaid through the end of the year. Once it's up, you'll have to find a place for all my photographic equipment, too."

"I will?"

"Of course."

"Let me guess. Since I'm keeping your money, I'm responsible for the consequences."

She offered a brilliant smile. "Finally. You understand."

A wry expression glinted in his dark eyes. "Sorry it took so long. Maybe it had something to do with the convoluted path I had to follow to get there." He didn't give her time to do more than wince before firing off his next question. "Explain something else for me."

"Do I have to?" There were far too many dangerous discussions for him to choose from, none of which she felt confident enough to tackle tonight. "You're a smart man, Gideon. Can't you figure out whatever it is by yourself?"

"Humor me." To her dismay, he left the couch and approached. If she had her camera she'd have called this snapshot, On the Prowl. She retreated behind the safety of his desk, the hem of her nightshirt fluttering around her thighs. "My secretary gave me some interesting information right before the Tylers arrived."

Oh, dear. Piper made a stab at appearing unconcerned. "Did she?"

"You sound nervous."

She deliberately edged her voice with a touch of irony. "Consider it an occupational hazard. Working for you tends to make me wary."

"A reasonable response."

Piper cleared her throat. "So what interesting information did Lindsey give you?"

"She said you'd applied for a job here a couple of weeks ago and that personnel was on the verge of hiring you. Is it true?"

Of all the various discoveries he could have made, this was the least dangerous. Thank heaven for that. "Yes. I sent in an application for employment," she readily confirmed. "Even if you hadn't gotten your hands on Jack Wiley's contract, we still would have met. We still might have worked together. And we still would have been forced to deal with past issues."

She didn't often see Gideon thrown off balance. But this had certainly done the trick. "Why? Why dredge it all up again? What's the point?"

"I didn't have any choice." Pain slipped into her voice despite her best efforts to prevent it. "Someone sent me an article about you. In the story they referred to you as 'Heartless Hart.' I had to find out if it was true."

"And if it was?"

"Then I planned to try to fix whatever went wrong."

He folded his arms across his chest, reminding her of an ancient warrior, hard and stalwart and resolute in his course of action. His stance warned that this wasn't a man to be influenced by the vagaries of women. "A rather ambitious project. How were you going to do that?"

She shrugged. "By finding your heart again."

His expression didn't soften as she'd hoped. "You think you know where to find it?"

"I suspect I'll discover that soon enough." She pried open one of the boxes. Her most recent photos were in plastic sleeves on top and she flipped through them until she found the picture she wanted. Next she pulled out a selection of professional shots. "Did I ever mention why I was such a popular wedding photographer?"

He didn't hesitate. "Because you're good."

She flashed him a teasing grin. "Well... That, too. But there's another reason." She fanned a series of plastic-encased photos across the desk. "I'm popular because I see beneath the surface. That's particularly true of the bridegrooms."

Gideon picked up the pictures, one by one. "These

are incredible." He flicked the bottommost one in her direction. "What's with this guy?"

"His is a failed marriage in the making."

He froze. "Failed?"

Piper grimaced. "Kevin doesn't want to be married. He just doesn't know it, yet. Unfortunately, neither does his wife, though that may have changed by now."

"And this one?" Gideon fired another across the desk toward her. "What's he looking at?"

"His bride. He's just seen her for the first time."

"That marriage is going to last," Gideon murmured.

"Yes, it will."

He released his breath in a gusty sigh. "Okay, Piper. What's your point?"

"My point is… My photos don't lie."

"And?"

"And I seem to have a knack for showing men at their most vulnerable."

Gideon's eyes darkened to obsidian. "Then it's fortunate that I don't have any vulnerabilities."

"Really?" She spun a photo back across the desk at him. It was the evening he'd been lying on the sofa in his darkened office, nursing a drink. She'd snapped the picture over his objections and now she saw why he'd resisted. "This picture says you do."

He didn't even look at it. "You're mistaken."

"Am I? Or are you simply hoping I'm wrong?"

His gaze remained fixed on hers. "Wishing I'm something—something I'm not, I should add—won't make it happen. Regardless of what that picture shows, I have no vulnerabilities. I won't allow myself any. You'd do well to remember that." He inclined his head toward the snapshot. "Take it. I don't want it."

Picking up the photo, she retreated from the desk. She'd study the picture in private and see if it didn't confirm her suspicions about Gideon. Not that she had any doubt. She knew this man better than she knew herself. But perhaps the photo would offer some insight on how best to reach him. At the door, she paused, a final question occurring to her. She didn't turn, afraid her expression would give her away.

"Were you really run out of Mill Run, or did you say that for Bill Tyler's benefit?" she asked.

"They ran me out."

Still she refused to look at him. "And...and the shotgun?"

"Present and accounted for, with—if you'll excuse the dramatics—an itchy finger on the trigger. You remember Murphy, don't you? I think he was praying I'd give him an excuse to pull that trigger."

She swiveled to face him at that, thoroughly alarmed. "You didn't give him an excuse?"

"I'm not that big a fool. I controlled my temper. Just."

Reassured, she turned to the subject that concerned her the most. "What about the note you sent me?" she dared to question. "What did it say?"

"Piper—"

"Is it so much to ask, Gideon?"

His jaw clenched. "I told you to join me out by the old Miller place. You always loved that homestead, even though it was little better than a ruin. It seemed the perfect meeting spot for my purposes."

"Why did you want to meet there?"

His hands folded into fists. "Next time read your notes and you wouldn't have to ask."

"Gideon, please."

The words came grudgingly. "I begged you to leave town with me."

"Is that all?" she whispered.

He shook his head, his gaze as dark and bleak as she'd ever seen them. "I asked you to marry me."

For a second she couldn't catch her breath, couldn't think, couldn't react. Tears she'd sworn she'd never shed filled her eyes. She heard an agonized sound, almost imperceptible, and to her horror realized it came from her. She had to leave—*now*—before she lost complete control.

"Piper?" His voice held a sharp demand she couldn't mistake.

She struggled to push a single word—anything at all—past the constriction in her throat. Something light and reassuring, something that would wipe away the dawning awareness in Gideon's gaze. But it was impossible. She backed up, holding out a hand in half plea, half rejection. The photo slipped from her fingers and fluttered to the floor. She stared at it for an endless moment, seeing the man she loved through a blur of tears.

She was right, came the helpless thought. Down deep where it counted, the Gideon Hart she'd known still lived. The photo confirmed that much. She clung to the knowledge, even as she felt the last bit of her control slipping away. She'd never been the sort of woman to turn and run. In fact, she'd always prided herself on facing up to even the most difficult circumstances. But for the first time in memory, she chose flight, needing to hide from Gideon's astute gaze, needing even more to confront the bitterness of a past she could never alter.

Escaping the room, she ran, leaving the photograph behind.

The door slammed closed behind Piper, and Gideon hesitated a minute before picking up the photograph. It was
the nighttime shot she'd taken after her meeting with the
owners of the jewelry companies and he stared at it,
exhaling roughly.

Damn.

It would seem he possessed one vulnerability, after
all. She'd caught him stretched out on the couch, one
knee bent, an arm tucked behind his head, nursing a
drink. Despite his posture, he didn't present the picture
of a man at ease, but one of a man in need. It was written
in every line of his face—a desperate hunger to possess.

There wasn't any question what he hungered for—or
whom. He was staring straight at his greatest need.

Piper.

Piper shivered. She didn't have much longer. The time
for absolute honesty was fast approaching. She'd known
this day would come, known it when she'd first read the
article about Gideon and realized she'd have to approach
him.

How would he react when he found out the rest of the
truth?

She curled into a tight ball. A few more days. Please.
Just a few more days to have him in her life again. To
say goodbye in her own way. To come to terms with the
past. She closed her eyes against the tears she'd been
unable to control.

Just a few more days.

*   *   *

Where the hell was she? It was nine o'clock at night, well past the time she should have gotten back from her appointment with Tyler. How long did it take to deliver bad news, anyway? Gideon stalked from his apartment down to his office. Snatching up the phone, he stabbed in the numbers connecting him with the security desk by the front door.

"Yes, Mr. Hart?"

"Has she returned, yet?"

"If you're referring to Ms. Montgomery, no, sir, she hasn't entered the building."

"Let me know when she arrives."

"Certainly, sir."

Dropping the receiver onto the cradle, he yanked at the tie anchored at his throat. He couldn't think in these clothes. They constricted his thoughts as thoroughly as his body. They always had. He'd never been a suit-and-tie sort of man. At times like this, that fact came home with a vengeance. He wasn't a native of the business world. And though he'd made a place in it, he'd never felt at home. As a result, he'd learned to compensate. Whenever he had serious decisions to make, he stripped down so he could breathe, so his mind could breathe, as well. Ripping off his shirt, he kicked his shoes to one side. The minute he was barefoot, he padded to the window and stared, unseeing, at the brightly lit city.

Why had she done it? Why had she interfered? She had to know he'd find out, that he'd be forced to act. What was this compulsive need of hers to put herself in the middle of places she didn't belong? And why did he keep protecting her every time she did?

The phone on his desk emitted a soft burr. He ignored it, knowing it had to be security warning him of Piper's arrival. He took a deep breath, hoping to bring himself under control before she reached his office. It wouldn't be easy. Not when his anger competed with a desire so strong it took every ounce of self-possession to keep his hands off her.

A few minutes later, the doors rattled and he heard Piper's muffled voice lifted in complaint. "...open when I tell you to open. Give me trouble again and I'll introduce you to the pointy end of my good friend, Mr. Ax." She tumbled into the office, her Leica swinging from the strap she'd slung over her shoulder. She blinked in surprise when she saw him standing at the window. "Oh, hello, Gideon. Sorry I'm late."

"I've been waiting for you."

"That's very sweet of—"

"It's not sweet. It's business." He slowly approached, knowing it was a mistake to get too close to her, but unable to resist. "Did you think I wouldn't find out, that someone wouldn't tell me what you'd done?"

She actually had the nerve to stick her chin out at him. "Hoped, might be a better word."

"Explain why you did it." The words held a cold bite.

"Certainly." She gave the matter some thought for a moment, before releasing a chagrined sigh. "Maybe you better tell me which bit of business I'd hoped you wouldn't find out about."

"There's more than one?"

She winced at the hint of roar in his voice. "It's possible. I'm new at this job. Heaven only knows how many mistakes I could have made."

"I'm not talking about a mistake." He found himself stepping closer, close enough to pick up the faintest hint of her perfume. "I'm talking about your conversation with the jewelers."

She regarded him warily. "Oh. That."

"Yes. That."

"I don't know why you're upset. I delivered your message. I told them you were still bent on deconstructing."

"You also told them to fight me!"

She dismissed that with a shrug. "It was a reasonable suggestion. You were the one who told me they'd gotten into trouble by refusing to cooperate. All I said was that if they banded together, they might be able to find a way out of their predicament."

"Don't you get it?" he bit out. "I don't want them to find a way out of their predicament."

"Of course I get it." A hint of annoyance sparked in her eyes. "They were the ones who didn't understand how determined you are, not me. It wasn't like I could give them any tangible assistance. All I could do was offer a little advice."

"But you would have helped if you could."

"Absolutely. I like helping people."

A final step brought him up against her and he cupped her shoulders, unable to resist putting his hands on her. "Then help me."

With a nearly inaudible sigh she fit herself to his angles. "Help you make things right, you mean?"

He expelled his breath in a harsh laugh, but didn't release her. Couldn't release her. Not when her mouth hovered so near his own. Not when her heartbeat marched with his. Not when her softness and light filled all the dark, hard places in his soul. "You never give up, do you?"

"Never. Come on, Gideon. You want to help them. Admit it."

"I want those businesses."

Her eyes burned with a desperate passion, a passion that had nothing to do with lust and everything to do with the depth of her conviction. "At any cost?"

"Yes."

The passion now filled her voice, ringing with unswerving determination. "No matter who it hurts?"

"Stay out of the way and you won't get hurt."

She was a flame in his arms, fierce and painfully brilliant. He exulted in what she'd become in the years they'd been apart, even as it saddened him that he hadn't witnessed that final growth. "I won't let you harm them, Gideon," she warned. "And I won't let you harm the man you were meant to be by taking them down."

"You can't stop me."

They'd wasted enough time on talk. There were other, more important matters that needed his attention. He lowered his head at the same instant as she lifted her mouth to meet his. Before he could take what he wanted so desperately, the double doors slammed against the walls and a man charged across the office.

"You son of a bitch! Take your filthy hands off her!"

Gideon reacted instinctively. Pivoting on one heel he swept Piper deeper into the protective darkness of the room and clear of the immediate threat. In the same motion, he slammed the heel of his palm square into the center of the invader's chest. It took him precisely that long to realize he'd taken down Spencer. The knowledge should have brought an immense amount of satisfaction. Instead he had the gut-level certainty that he'd chosen precisely the wrong actions—at least as far as Piper was concerned.

Sure enough, she balled up her fist and socked him in the arm, at a guess doing more injury to herself than to him. "You idiot! What's with the Jackie Chan imitation? For once in your life could you handle things with your head instead of your fists?"

"Doubtful," he admitted. How did he explain that he'd have done whatever necessary—no matter how combative or violent—to protect her? Hell, he couldn't even explain it to himself.

She turned her attention to the man sprawled on the ground. "Darn it, Spencer! What are you doing here?"

To Gideon's immense satisfaction, it took Spencer three tries to get the words out. "Saving you."

"Now why does that sound familiar, not to mention totally unnecessary?"

Slowly Spencer gained his feet, fury mingling with his pain. "Look at him!" He glared at Gideon. "He's half naked. The lights are out. And he was touching you. What was I supposed to think?"

She folded her arms across her chest. "Yes, I can see why you'd need to attack him over that."

"I didn't attack him, I—"

"You charged me like some sort of demented bull," Gideon interrupted.

"I meant to do a hell of a lot more than charge you. I meant to knock you on your ass." With a groan, Spencer bent at the waist, resting his hands on his knees as he struggled to draw a deep breath. "Give me a minute and I'll see if I can't get it right this time."

Amusement vied with a reluctant admiration. "You

haven't won any of our other fights,'' Gideon observed.
"What makes you think you're going to win this one?"

"I've had more practice."

"So I've noticed."

The hint of sarcasm provoked an instant reaction. If
Piper hadn't stepped between them, Spencer would have
charged again. A shame, really. Gideon would have relished another excuse to imitate Jackie Chan.

Spencer must have read his intent because instead of
attacking, he draped a protective arm around his sister.
"Let's go, Piper."

"She's not going anywhere. I haven't dismissed her,
yet."

The provocative words had the precise effect Gideon
had hoped. Disbelief glittered in Spencer's blue eyes and
he bristled with renewed masculine aggression. "What
the hell does that mean, 'dismissed'?"

"Just what it sounds like. As her employer, she has
to wait until I give her permission to leave." He allowed
that to sink in before continuing. "I haven't given it to
her, yet."

Spencer shook his head. "She doesn't work for you."

Gideon bared his teeth in a feral grin. He shouldn't
be enjoying this so much, but he was. "Flash bulletin,
Montgomery. She started this week."

"Then consider this her first *and* last week."

Piper slipped free of Spencer's grasp. "Has anyone
noticed that I'm still here?"

"We'll discuss that soon enough," her brother
snapped. "Why you're here… Why you shouldn't be…
And why you won't be coming here ever again."

"Cute. But I don't take orders from you."

"Only from me," Gideon goaded.

She turned on him, her expression revealing a protective streak as wide as his own. Once upon a time she'd have defended him with every bit as much passion. He shouldn't miss those days, but he did. "You're not helping," she complained.

"I'm not trying to help. You're not the one I want, if you'll remember."

Piper clutched her camera more tightly, but to his relief didn't pop off any shots. He didn't think he'd appreciate what the developed photos might reveal about his inner psyche—at least, her interpretation of what they revealed. She had a knack for sharing her impressions with a brutal frankness he could live without.

Her expression turned mutinous. "Oh, no, you don't. You're not going after my brother. Our agreement stands despite this latest wrinkle. Spencer was bound to find out about our arrangement at some point." She shot her brother a disgruntled look. "I hadn't expected it to be this soon. How *did* you find out, by the way?"

"I told him," Gideon volunteered. "Or perhaps I should say I told him just enough to get him on the next plane out of California."

She closed her eyes. "Of course. I should have known. How can you fully savor your revenge otherwise?"

"I couldn't."

"Someone tell me what's going on," Spencer demanded. *"Now."*

Piper sighed. "What has Gideon explained so far?"

"Obviously, not enough. Last night I get this crazy phone call from tough guy, here—" he gestured toward Gideon "—who warns me you're holed up in his apartment and if I were any sort of responsible brother, I'd get back to Denver and rescue you."

To Gideon's annoyance, Piper fixed him with a stare that had him shifting in place like a recalcitrant schoolboy. Hell. He knew that look. She thought there was some special significance to his actions, something—he almost choked—noble about his phoning Spencer. Well, there wasn't, other than as a convenient way to get his hands on her brother. Whatever ridiculous assumptions she was about to come up with to explain what a good guy he was were dead wrong, something he'd take pains to point out at the earliest opportunity.

"Last night must have really rattled you for you to go to so much trouble to get Spencer back here," she murmured. "Was it because of what happened at dinner with the Tylers or our late-night conversation?"

"I believe it was the fact that your bedroom door doesn't have any locks," he replied blandly.

"Ah. So it wasn't fear, but temptation." Amused exasperation gleamed in her eyes. "Very heroic of you to try to rescue me from a fate worse than death, especially considering it would have been at your hands."

"I haven't fallen so far from grace that I'd use you to even the score with your brother."

She planted her hands on her hips. "Did it ever occur to you that I might not want to be rescued?" she dared to suggest. "Or that, despite any temptation you might feel, we both know you'd never try to get even that way?"

He went nose to nose with her, allowing his annoyance to filter through to his voice. "Yes, it did occur to me that you might not want to be rescued. It's one of your most aggravating failings. You keep forgetting that I'm the villain of the piece, not the hero.''

She snapped her fingers. ''Oh, right. Silly me. I can't imagine how I could have made such an obvious mistake. How could I have confused you with anything other than a villain?'' She returned his glare with one of her own. ''Maybe it has something to do with the tights and cape you're wearing, not to mention the way you keep running interference anytime you think I might get hurt.''

He thrust a hand through his hair. Piper Montgomery was going to drive him utterly and completely insane—assuming she hadn't already. ''I've never yet met a woman in jeopardy who's so determined to tie herself to the railroad tracks and encourage the train to run over her instead of allowing herself to be swept to safety,'' he complained. He stabbed a finger in Spencer's direction. ''Even when I arrange for your rescue, you still don't appreciate it. Damned if you don't throw yourself back down on those tracks and flag the train again. And as for my using you to even the score with your brother, don't fool yourself. I'd have been in your room in a heartbeat last night.''

''What stopped you?''

Because I couldn't hurt you like that, he almost said. *Because once I'd made love to you, I wouldn't have been able to let you go again.* He clamped his jaws together, facing the unpalatable truth. No matter what had happened between them in the past, he couldn't deliberately harm her now. Worse, if he'd made love to her, not only wouldn't he have been able to let her go, he'd never have been able to take her brother apart. He glared at

Spencer. Dammit all, if he didn't get Piper out of the line of fire, he still might not be able to.

"Hell-o? Would someone *please* tell me what the devil is going on?" Spencer interrupted. "Why are you working for this SOB, Piper? And why the *hell* are you staying in his apartment? Have you lost every ounce of common sense?"

"Probably," she said in perfect seriousness.

Gideon folded his arms across his chest. Time to take over this little discussion. He wanted Piper away from ground zero as quickly as possible, while sticking Spencer square in the middle of it. Then maybe he could get down to some serious revenge-taking. "It's quite simple. I bought out your note."

"Note?" Spencer frowned in confusion. "What note?"

Piper nudged him with her elbow. "You know. *The* note."

"That's right," Gideon said. "*The* note. Your contract with Jack Wiley, remember? I recently bought it from his estate and I'm calling it due."

He had to give Spencer credit. Once he caught on, he caught on fast. Shock swiftly gave way to a blistering anger. "You son of a—"

"That's getting a bit redundant," Gideon baited. "Can't you come up with anything more inventive?"

Instantly Piper jumped into the fray. "Calm down, Spence. I'm handling it."

Would the woman never learn to keep clear of his affairs? Gideon wondered, thoroughly livid. Doubtful, given her track record to date. "Stay out of this," he warned.

"No, I won't stay out of it." She kept her attention

focused on her brother. "Gideon can't take the mill if we give him something of equal value. It's in the contract."

Impotent fury gathered in Spencer's eyes. "We don't have any other assets. What the hell can we give him that's worth anything close to the value of the mill?"

"I am."

CHAPTER SEVEN

THE simple words hung between them for an impossibly long minute, impacting on Gideon like a blow. Maybe Piper's comment hit *him* far harder than Spencer because he'd never realized the truth until that moment. She *was* worth more than the mill. His distraction cost him. With a roar of fury, Spencer launched himself at Gideon, catching him by surprise.

The two of them slammed together, clipping Piper's shoulder before crashing to the floor. She fell against his desk, the sound of shattering glass far louder than her soft gasp of pain. But it was that minute sound that brought Gideon to his senses. All thoughts of rearranging Spencer's face fled the instance he realized she might be hurt. He struggled to free himself.

"Pipsqueak?"

Spencer shoved Gideon aside and gained his feet first. "Piper? Honey, are you all right?"

Her camera had fallen to the floor and she slowly knelt beside it, her back to them. "I'd like you to go, Spencer," she said far too quietly.

"No way," he protested. "I'm not going anywhere without you."

"Yes. Yes, you are."

He held out a hand in appeal. "Piper, please. Don't do this. You can't still want to defend him. Not after all this time. And not after what occurred five years ago."

"He doesn't know. He doesn't know about the fight and its aftermath."

"That's bull!"

"I'm telling you, he was never told." She spared a quick glance over her shoulder. The starkness in her eyes nearly sent Gideon into a frenzy. If he hadn't been positive Spencer would attack again, he'd have been all over Piper in order to find out what was causing such agony. "He doesn't know what happened any more than I knew about his being run out of town."

Gideon caught Spencer by the arm, forcing him away from Piper. "You really didn't tell her I was kicked out of Mill Run?"

"Of course not. I'd have been a fool to." He shook off the hold with a quick, impatient shrug. "She doesn't lie. Or has it been so many years you've forgotten?"

No, Gideon hadn't forgotten. He'd simply resisted believing. It had been far easier to think she'd ultimately sided with her brother and allowed the sheriff to force him to leave than to consider the alternative—that she'd never loved him in the first place. That what had meant the world to him had been nothing more than a brief, meaningless fling for her. "Why? Why keep the truth from her?"

"You were gone," Spencer explained grudgingly. "There was no point in her hearing all the details. And after what you'd done to her, I didn't think she could handle—"

"You were wrong to keep it from me, Spence," Piper cut in. There was a desperate roughness to her voice, an unmistakable undertone of pain. "I thought Gideon had left me. I thought he didn't care."

Spencer started toward her and Gideon shifted to

block his way. "Don't even think about it, Montgomery. The only way you touch her is by going through me."

"Don't tempt me!" He returned his attention to his sister. "Piper, listen to me. I'm sorry I didn't tell you the truth about Hart, okay? But that doesn't change anything. He wants revenge and he'll take it anyway he can, even if it's through you."

"You're wrong. He'd never deliberately hurt me."

Spencer swore in frustration. "Don't be a fool. That's precisely what he'll do. No matter what you think, he *doesn't* care."

"Maybe not now. But he deserves the truth about the past and I'm going to make sure he gets it. Then if he still wants revenge, I'll let the two of you sort it out."

Her determination must have finally penetrated because Spencer's shoulders sagged in defeat. "How long?"

"Just a few days. That's all I'm asking. I need time to explain everything in my own way."

Gideon refused to stay quiet another minute. There were nuances to this encounter that he was missing. He felt like a player without a rule book or a clue as to what game they were playing, and he didn't like it one little bit. "Explain what, Piper? What are you two keeping from me?"

She didn't answer, instead curling into a tighter ball.

Something was wrong and he suspected it had little to do with a broken camera lens. Gideon jerked his head toward the door. "Get out, Montgomery."

"Please go, Spence," she begged. "I'll call you later and give you the details about the money we owe."

"Piper—"

"*Please.*"

Gideon had never heard her so close to the edge before. Without a word, he crossed his office and opened the doors. His look warned that he'd use physical force, if necessary, to eject Spencer. Piper's brother hesitated a moment longer before turning and following.

"Hurt her and it'll be the last thing you ever do" came his parting shot.

It took every scrap of Gideon's self-control not to lay hands on Spencer again. "If you don't want her hurt, fight your own damn battles. I want that mill. Give it to me and she's all yours."

Spencer inclined his head in acknowledgment. To Gideon's surprise, he added in an undertone, "I didn't tell her the truth about why you left town because she would have gone chasing after you."

"It wasn't your decision."

"I made it my decision. You were bad news then, and you're even worse news now." Spencer invaded Gideon's space, his statement low and intense. "Just so it's clear between us, I don't believe for a minute that you didn't know the full extent of the damage you left in your wake."

"For the last time… I didn't burn your mill," Gideon stated through clenched teeth.

"I'm not talking about the damage you did to the mill. You think I give a damn about that in comparison to my sister?" A smoldering fury settled over Spencer. "The only reason I'm leaving now is because Piper insists and I'd do anything for my sister. But she's all that's stopping me from putting you down so hard you wouldn't be able to get up in a month of Sundays. I'm also telling you flat out. You're not getting the mill and you're definitely not getting my sister. I won't have you ruin either one. Not again.''

With that Spencer disappeared through the doors. Gideon closed them with more force than necessary and glanced at Piper. She remained hunched on the floor beside his desk, her back to him, cradling her camera in her lap. Aw, hell. This couldn't be good. He was at her side in two seconds flat. Crouching behind her, he folded his arms around her in a comforting embrace and hugged her to his chest.

"I'm sorry, sweetheart. I didn't mean for your camera to get broken. How bad is it?''

She shuddered in his grasp, her breath coming in short, shallow pants. "I need a towel, please. A damp towel, if you don't mind.''

The starkness of her request left him feeling as though he'd been sucker-punched. "What's wrong?''

"Gideon…please.''

The words were barely audible, but they had him instantly reacting. He carefully released her and charged into the bathroom adjoining his office. Ripping a towel from the bar, he thrust it under the faucet. A half-dozen swift strides returned him to her side. He saw it then. She held her left hand clasped tightly to her right arm. His office was too dark to distinguish color very well, but even in the subdued lighting he could tell her fingers were bright with blood.

A single, brutal word escaped before he gritted his teeth and stooped beside her, pressing the damp towel to her arm to stem the flow of blood. "What the hell happened?'' he demanded.

"It was my fault. I tried to catch the camera before it dropped and I slipped against your desk. My arm caught the corner. I didn't want Spencer to see I'd been injured. He...he wouldn't have taken it too well.''

''My *desk* cut you?''

She managed a broken laugh. ''Apparently some of your trophies are even more dangerous than the man who collects them.''

He flinched at the comment. ''Dammit! I can't see what I'm doing. Come on. Let's get you into the bathroom.''

He didn't wait for her to stand, but simply scooped her up and carted her into the connecting room. Setting her on her feet, he turned on the water and eased her arm beneath the faucet. Then he gently pulled away the towel.

''How bad is it?'' she asked, refusing to look. There wasn't any expression in her voice, but she'd turned deathly white.

''You didn't cut an artery, if that's what you're asking.'' How he managed to sound so steady and in control, he'd never know. ''But we need to get you to the hospital so they can stitch this up.''

''*No!* No hospital.''

''Be sensible, Piper.''

''No hospital,'' she repeated. Her refusal contained a quality he'd never heard before, warning that she was far more upset than he'd first thought. ''Clean it with soap and stick a bandage on it. Tomorrow I'll see the doctor in his office. But I'm not going to the hospital.''

''I've got news for you. You're not going to wait until tomorrow to see a doctor, and that's final.''

She began to shake. ''Drop the tough guy act. You can't bark orders and expect me to obey.''

''As your employer, that's precisely what I can do.

But if it makes you feel any better, I have an in at the local emergency room. Lucy—do you remember my younger sister?''

He'd succeeded in momentarily distracting her. ''Of course I remember her. When I was little I thought you two were twins.''

''Well, she's an ER doctor now. I'll give her a call and have her meet us at the hospital. She owes me a favor or two.''

''I still don't want to— Ouch! That stings.''

He dabbed cautiously at the wound. ''Sorry. I didn't mean to hurt you.''

''Oh, shoot.'' Her breathing grew shallow and rapid. ''Gideon?''

''What is it, pipsqueak?''

''I really do apologize.''

If the circumstances had been different, he'd have found her formality amusing. ''Hell, woman. What do you have to apologize for?''

''I'm either going to get sick or faint. Maybe both.''

He should have realized how bad off she was a lot sooner. Wrapping a clean towel around her arm, he pulled her close and lowered her to the tile floor, cradling her against his chest. She fit as perfectly as she always had, as though she'd been born for his embrace. ''Rest for a minute. Then I'll call Lucy. She doesn't live too far away.''

''I don't want—''

''We're going to the hospital and that's final.'' Piper didn't answer, but simply turned her face into his shoulder, a sigh shuddering through her. He'd never known she had a fear of hospitals. Perhaps it had something to do with her mother's death. He vaguely recalled it had involved cancer. No doubt that sort of illness would have required lengthy hospital stays that would have had an adverse effect on a young girl. "I'm going to carry you to the couch now. Then I'll give my sister a call."

Within thirty minutes they were at the hospital, the three of them closeted in a small cubicle. "Of course you did the right thing bringing her here," Lucy groused. "I can't believe you even bothered discussing it. That's not like you."

"We're in shock," Gideon offered blandly.

"Right." Lucy dismissed him with an irritated shrug and gave Piper a professional smile. "It's not deep, fortunately. Only a couple of stitches necessary. I'll also update your tetanus shot. I assume Gideon can keep an eye on you tonight?"

"Yes."

Lucy groaned. "I was afraid you'd say that. But if my brother wants to make a fool of himself over you again, that's his business. I can't stop him."

"That's enough, Lucy." Gideon cut in. "I'm dealing with the situation."

She gave his bare torso and low-slung jeans a pointed look. "Yeah, I see how you're dealing with it. She made your life a misery once, why in the world would you let her do it again?"

"Would you like to put the stitches in crooked?" Piper offered.

Lucy stared in confusion. "What?"

"Would it make you feel better if I let you put the stitches in crooked? Or you can forget the stitches altogether and let it scar."

"I'd never do that," Lucy protested. "I try to help people, not hurt them."

"And I'd never hurt your brother. Not deliberately. I never have and I never will." Piper's gaze didn't waver. "I didn't know your brother was run out of town. If I had, perhaps these past five years would have ended differently."

Gideon went very still, her comment prompting a memory. *He doesn't know. He doesn't know about the fight and its aftermath.* Once before he'd had the impression he was playing a game without having all the rules. The feeling grew stronger, clawing at him with an urgency he couldn't ignore. Piper's injury had prevented him from demanding an explanation. But one way or another, he'd force the truth from her. And he'd do it tonight.

"Fix her up," he ordered. "I want to get out of here."

Lucy's mouth tightened. "No problem." It didn't take long to close and bandage the wound. The minute she'd finished, she gave Gideon a list of instructions. Standing to leave, she glanced at Piper and released her breath in a long sigh. "Fair warning. I'm going to hold you to that promise not to hurt my brother. Mess it up and you'll have some very angry sisters to deal with."

Piper smiled. "My brother said more or less the same thing to Gideon. Maybe we should all get together and compare notes. I'll bet we have more in common than you might think."

Lucy returned her smile with less reluctance than she'd shown to date. "I'll give you this much... Leaving Mill Run was the best thing that ever happened to us. We owe you for that, if nothing else."

On the car trip home, Piper remained strangely quiet. Even on the elevator ride to his apartment, she refused to be drawn into any discussions. It wasn't until they were in the living room, recovering from their ordeal with a small splash of brandy that she turned to Gideon. "What did Lucy mean by that? About leaving Mill Run being the best thing that ever happened to you?"

He hesitated, cradling the snifter between his hands. This wasn't a story he'd planned to repeat to anyone. But there'd been enough secrets between them. She deserved the truth. "After I was thrown in jail, there was no one to protect my mother and sisters from my father."

She stared in horror. "Oh, Gideon—"

"Don't feel too bad. It finally gave my mother the incentive she needed to gather up the girls and leave. Until then, they had nowhere to go. When I was run out of town, they followed. Somehow we muddled through, though that first year almost destroyed us."

He saw the tears come, like dark clouds marring a perfect blue sky. He found the sight unexpectedly wrenching. "It was a long time ago, Piper," he said gently.

She swiped at the tears that fell. "You say that like it's over." Her response had a fierce, impatient edge. "If it were, you wouldn't still hold a grudge. What happened back then changed something fundamental inside of you. And look at the path you've chosen as a result."

He fought against an irrational surge of anger. "That path has provided my family with a livelihood they wouldn't have otherwise enjoyed. It put all my sisters through college, paid for Lucy's medical training and gave my mother the first home she's ever known. Before that she'd lived her life in squalor, barely subsisting inside of a run-down trailer that wasn't fit for pigs. It also gave me the drive to make more of myself than I could have if I'd stayed in Mill Run.'' He swallowed the last of his brandy and set the snifter aside, the glass clattering discordantly against the wooden table. ''And it showed me what happens when you allow yourself to be vulnerable. Vulnerabilities make you weak.''

''Was I one of your vulnerabilities, Gideon?'' she demanded. ''Was our love? Did that make you weak?''

He stood and crossed to the windows, staring out at the city nightscape for a long moment. ''You were my only vulnerability,'' he confessed. ''And my greatest weakness.''

''And you won't make that mistake again, will you?''

''Not a chance.'' He glanced over his shoulder, fixing her with an implacable gaze. ''I want to know what you've been keeping from me, Piper. Now. What information do you and Spencer have about the day of the fight that I lack? What are you hiding?''

He could see her debating how best to answer. Then she joined him at the window, standing dangerously close. Desire swirled between them, driven by forces beyond his control or resistance. It was as though a connection existed on some alternate plane, as though some primal awareness formed between them whenever they were together. He could feel the ancient weaving begin, the swift formation of silken bonds that shimmered with a primitive imperative to join. To mate. To form a necessary whole from emotions which had remained separate and incomplete for far too long.

''All right. I'll explain everything, but I'm not sure you'll appreciate the explanation,'' she warned.

''Let me worry about that.'' The lingering traces of a hospital odor clung to her and his frustration grew. Or perhaps the unique bonding he sensed between them added to his distress. She shouldn't smell like a medicine cabinet. He knew her distinctive perfume and it wasn't this. If he had his way, she'd never carry this scent again. "Answer me, Piper."

With a reluctant sigh, she slipped her hands around his neck. "No, Gideon, don't move," she warned the instant he reached for her wrists. "You'll reopen my cut."

He stood rigid within her embrace. "What are you doing?"

"Answering your question…in my own way." She smiled up at him with an invasive warmth that overran every barrier he possessed. "Or has it been so long that you're no longer familiar with this mode of communication?"

She pressed herself against him. She was so soft. So feminine. So imbued with a warmth of body and spirit. He fought to hold perfectly still instead of molding her close as he'd have liked. He clenched his hands at his sides instead of filling them with her lush curves and exploring all that he'd once known so intimately. Her actions brought home an unpalatable fact. No matter what he claimed to the contrary, she remained his only vulnerability and greatest weakness.

"I seem to remember your using this method last time you tried to avoid my questions. It worked that time." The words grated. "It's not going to work again."

"I know. But let it work for a minute longer. Please, Gideon. Give me this one, brief indulgence and then I'll answer your question."

He found it impossible to refuse her request, not when he craved to have her mouth beneath his, her lips spread in welcome. Intense desire swept over him and every masculine instinct urged him to seize what he wanted, as though she were a business acquisition to be taken by force. Instead he cautiously cupped her face and stole a kiss. Gently, tenderly. Rather than demanding a reaction, he found himself coaxing it. And when he'd won the softest of sighs and the most generous of responses, he found himself doing something he'd have sworn he'd lost the ability to do.

He gave back with all that he had.

She held him for a moment longer, as giving as he'd tried to be, succeeding far better because she was more generous by nature. A different quality entered the kiss and it took him a moment to realize what had changed. And then it hit him. He couldn't explain how he knew, but he had a gut-level certainty that she was saying goodbye—and that was why she'd kissed him before offering the answers he craved. Because once she explained it would somehow change their relationship. Suddenly he didn't want the answers, couldn't even remember the questions.

"No," he muttered against her mouth. "Don't stop now."

"We have to. I made a promise and I'm going to keep it."

"Piper—"

She took a deep, steadying breath. "Thank you for helping me tonight."

"It doesn't have to end," he insisted.

"Yes. Yes, it does."

He couldn't explain the desperation he felt. Desperation suggested an unfulfilled need. And he knew better than to need anything or anyone. Hadn't he told Piper that he wouldn't leave himself that open again?

"At least spend the night with me. Let me make love to you. We can talk in the morning."

"No. We have to finish our discussion tonight. I might lose my nerve by morning." She escaped his arms with a reluctance even he couldn't mistake and crossed to the doorway leading to the bedrooms. There she paused. "I never answered your question earlier. And you deserve to know."

"Know what?"

Her throat moved as she swallowed. "You asked what Spence and I were keeping from you. What we knew about the fight you didn't."

"And?"

"During the fight I fell off the embankment and was injured." She shrugged as though it were no big deal. "That's why I didn't realize you'd been arrested. Or that you'd been run out of town. I was in the hospital."

A minute later he heard the soft click of her bedroom door closing.

Gideon couldn't sleep. He kept hearing Piper's words. *During the fight I fell off the embankment and was injured. That's why I didn't realize you'd been arrested. Or that you'd been run out of town. I was in the hospital.* There was more. Far more than she'd told him. He could tell from her expression and from the bleakness in her eyes. And he suspected he knew what it was.

Escaping his rumpled bed, he climbed into his jeans and headed downstairs to his office. Rescuing Piper's camera from the floor, he examined the damage. The lens had shattered and would have to be replaced. He'd leave a message for his secretary to get it taken care of first thing in the morning, even if she had to have the new part flown in overnight from Germany.

After cleaning up the shards of glass, he made his way back upstairs. Silence reigned, the lack of sound oppressive. For some reason, he wanted to throw things, to pound the pavement in a mind-numbing run, to utilize every muscle in his body in the sort of hard, physical labor he'd known during his days in Old Mill Run. Anything that would drown out the voices in his head. Anything that would leave him too exhausted to think. Instead he paced from room to room until he found himself standing outside of Piper's bedroom, drawn by forces he refused to acknowledge. The pull proved irresistible.

Grasping the knob, he shoved the door inward, light from the hallway vanquishing the darkness. It spilled across the carpet, rushing toward the bed where it extinguished the last of its radiance on the form curled beneath the covers. He could tell from her breathing that she slept, her injured arm propped on a pillow.

A painful tightness closed his throat. Why did she have to be so foolhardy? She shouldn't have put herself in the middle of two men bent on doing serious physical damage to each other. She'd been hurt because she had a ridiculous need to protect Spencer—as though her brother required protection. Gideon shut his eyes, acknowledging the bitter truth. Rationalizations wouldn't work any longer. He'd wanted a confrontation, thirsted for the opportunity to tell Spencer his plans for revenge face-to-face. And he'd gotten that opportunity. But at whose expense?

Dammit all! What the hell had he done?

When had his need for vengeance become so all-consuming that it allowed him to harm the woman he'd once loved more than anything in this world? He approached the bed and gazed down at her, a slight smile easing the rigid muscles knotting his jaw. He'd adored this woman from boyhood and despite the changes he'd undergone—changes that clearly distressed her—she'd remained constant. In fact, there was little he could see that was different.

She was still as strong-willed as she was generous, and just as determined to battle for the underdog as she'd always been. Even her hair had stayed the same, the thick blond strands as ruler-edge straight as ever. He gathered up a handful. And it still had the softest texture he'd ever felt. His smile faded as he allowed her hair to sift through his fingers.

Tomorrow. Tomorrow he'd get the rest of the truth from her. He'd find out how she fell from the embankment and ended up in the hospital. Until then, he'd stay well away from her before he did something they'd both regret.

Silently he crossed to the door.

"Gideon?"

Piper sat up and stared in confusion. Gideon stood in the doorway of the bedroom, his back to her. At the sound of her voice, he stiffened, his sudden tension communicated itself in the rigid set of his shoulders and the stiffness of his spine.

"Go back to sleep," he told her without turning around.

"What are you doing here?"

"Checking to make sure you're all right."

"I'm fine." But he wasn't. Something was very wrong. "What is it, Gideon? What's happened?"

Still he didn't face her. "Nothing you need to worry about. Go back to sleep," he repeated.

She drew her knees to her chest. "You can't fool me. I know you too well. Something's upset you. Is it your fight with Spencer?"

He turned then, the light stabbing across his profile for a brief moment. It betrayed the torment in his dark eyes and the grim set of his jaw. Furrows cut a path from the corners of his mouth to the harshly arched cheekbones. "Not the fight. It's the results of the fight."

"My arm?" she asked gently.

"You shouldn't have put yourself in the middle. I warned you about that."

"Yes, you did," she promptly agreed. "My mistake. You once said I had to be the only woman foolish enough to wade into a fistfight and risk my own well-being out of concern for the brawlers. I guess this proves it."

"Don't make light of it!"

Good heavens. He really was upset. "How am I supposed to react?" she asked reasonably. "How was I supposed to react when you and Spencer started fighting?"

"By staying out of it."

"Ah. But you don't understand."

He glared for an instant before releasing his breath in a slow sigh. "Okay, Piper. I'll bite. What don't I understand?"

"I couldn't stay out of it. How could I? You're the two men I love most in all this world."

The words were stated with breathtaking candor and Gideon flinched as though he'd been struck. "You can't. Not any longer."

She simply laughed. "Of course I can."

"Spencer, sure. But not—" His throat moved convulsively and he shook his head.

"I fell in love with you when I was eight years old. It was when you promised to protect me, promised that no one would ever hurt me again. You gave me your word of honor, remember?"

"You're not eight anymore." His words grated. "And I broke my word long ago."

"Not deliberately. You protected me as long as you could. I didn't expect more than that."

He banged his fist against the doorjamb. "Dammit, Piper! Stop trying to make me into something I'm not. I don't know the man you keep describing, but it isn't me."

"I know who you are. It's you who's forgotten."

He swept that aside with a wave of his hand. "Fine," he said wearily. "Believe what you like, if it makes you feel better. All I ask is that you get out of my way. Spencer and I can take things from here."

"Not a chance. Neither of you are rational about this issue. I'm not going to let you take Spence down, any more than I'm going to let him harm you. There has to be an alternative and I intend to find it."

"Piper—"

"Next subject, Gideon."

He looked like he intended to say more, but then he shrugged. "As long as you're awake, I need to ask you something."

Uh-oh. The glitter in his eyes warned that she wouldn't like this topic any better than the last. "Tonight? It can't wait until morning?"

"No, it can't wait. Not if I want to get any sleep."

It didn't take much guesswork to figure out what was

troubling him. She gave in to the inevitable. "Okay. Ask your question."

"You said you fell off the ridge by the mill." He took a deep breath as though steeling himself for her response. "How?"

She gave him a final out. "You really don't want to know."

"It was my fault, wasn't it? I don't know how or why, but—" A muscle bunched in his jaw and she could see him struggle to push the question past clenched teeth. "But somehow I'm responsible, aren't I?"

"It was my fault."

"How?"

"I tried to stop the fight, same as tonight. Sound familiar?" Her mouth tilted into a wry smile. "I'm beginning to suspect this is an aspect of my personality that needs some work."

His brow creased and she could tell he was struggling to recall the details. Finally he shook his head. "No, you weren't anywhere near the fight at the mill."

"Not at first, because I couldn't get to you. There were too many people in the way and they wouldn't let me through. But then you broke through the circle, remember? Everyone scattered."

"How could I forget? That's when someone knocked me off my feet. I cracked two ribs."

"Oh, Gideon." She hadn't known that part. Unfortunately a lot of the specifics had escaped her notice. "How in the world did you manage to keep going?"

"I didn't have any choice." He shifted position and the light played across the drawn planes of his face, warning of emotions kept rigidly in check. "Tell me the rest, Piper. How did you get hurt?"

"When you stood up, I knew from your expression that either you or Spencer was going down and whichever one of you it ended up being would get badly hurt." She lowered her voice. "You two were so close to the drop-off. I was terrified you might be killed."

"Finish it, Piper!"

The words came in a desperate rush. "I made a terrible mistake. I grabbed your arm. You didn't know it was me. I'm sure you thought I was the person who'd tripped you."

"I vaguely remember someone grabbing me right before I knocked Spencer out. I shook him—you—off."

"I lost my footing. That's when I fell."

CHAPTER EIGHT

GIDEON swore with such guttural fury that Piper flinched. Then he was across the room, sweeping her into his arms. "There were rocks down there. Sharp rocks."

She made an unsuccessful stab at humor. "So I discovered."

"I'm sorry. I'm so sorry."

"You didn't know it was me. And it was over a long time ago."

"How bad was it?"

Just thinking about those dark days caused helpless tears to threaten. She didn't dare let Gideon see them. She blinked hard, fighting to keep all hint of pain from her voice. "Don't think about it," she whispered. "I don't."

"How bad?"

She didn't know how to answer him, what words would reassure him when they hadn't succeeded in reassuring her. Silence seemed her only option. He must have read some of what she was feeling in her eyes. He eased her back against the pillows, gently subduing her instinctive attempt to escape. Slowly, with an implacable determination she didn't have a hope of fighting, he released the buttons of her nightshirt, one after another. She caught at his hands, trying to stop him, but he wouldn't be deterred. He was too strong, too purposeful. Sweeping the thin cotton from her shoulders, he examined her. She didn't attempt to hide herself from his gaze, but remained motionless, naked and exposed.

His breathing changed the instant he found what he sought, the give and take acquiring a harsh, shallow quality. Gideon cupped her shoulder, tracing the thin, silvery line that tattooed her in a sicklelike curve. "Did you break your arm?"

"My...my collarbone."

"Is there more?"

She clenched her teeth and waited. Tossing the shirt aside, he shifted their positions so they lay directly in the path of the light filtering in from the hallway. It gilded her in gold, pitiless in what it exposed. She stared at the ceiling, the tears she tried so hard to suppress sliding from the corners of her eyes and dampening the hair at her temples. The thundering of his heartbeat filled her ears, his raspy groan an expression of such agony she didn't think she could bear it. Then he touched her again, his fingertip finding the jagged scar at its starting point high on her hip. Without a word he followed it, inch by excruciating inch until he reached its ending point, low on her belly.

Her breath escaped in a shuddering gasp at the intimate touch. No one had seen that scar, other than her doctors. But Gideon was intent on exploring every bit of it. When she didn't think she could stand another second, he lowered his head. His hair brushed across her stomach, his breath gusting on her skin. And then his mouth closed over the scar. A quiver started deep inside, directly beneath his lips, spreading a warmth that had once been a vital part of her life.

"Gideon!" His name burst from her, a plea for something she didn't dare put into words.

"I did this to you."

"It was an accident."

"I put these marks on your body." He lifted his head and stared at her. If she could have looked away she would have. The frenzied bitterness in his eyes was beyond anything she'd ever seen before, his pain even greater than her own. "If I could transfer them to my own flesh, I would."

She believed him. "I know you'd never deliberately hurt me."

"Not then."

"And not now." The words came without doubt or hesitation.

He traced the scar a final time. "Right now hurting you is the furthest thing from my mind." Devastation scored his face. "I'm so sorry, pipsqueak."

Piper reacted instinctively. Closing her arms around him, she gathered him close, simply holding him. There weren't any words that would comfort him. At least none that had successfully comforted her. She'd dreaded this moment, when he'd find out how their worlds had been destroyed that day by the mill. It had been one of the reasons she'd stayed away from him for five lonely years. But no longer. He needed her every bit as much as she needed him. The time had come to heal old wounds.

"We all made mistakes, Gideon. But they're passed. What we have to decide is how we go on from here."

"Let me show you how...."

A fierce resolution settled into his expression and he communicated his intent slowly, without words. His mouth closed over hers with delicious insistence. The touch felt hesitant, almost experimental, yet filled with a tenderness she'd thought lost to him. A freshness invaded the kiss, a tentative sampling, as though he were tasting something untried and novel. She'd never experienced such an erotic sensation—a virginal newness combined with a sensual familiarity. It reminded her vividly of their first time together when forever had stretched before them in unlimited possibilities.

He must have thought the same. "Do you remember?" he whispered. "Do you remember the first night we made love?"

She hadn't forgotten a single moment. How could she? Her world had changed that night. He'd turned girlish fantasies into a reality she'd kept sheltered in her heart to this day. Whether he realized it or not they were forever joined, and part of her would remain in his possession until the end of their days. "You didn't want it to happen," she reminded.

"You were too young. I shouldn't have touched you." Then, as though in unconscious denial of his own words, his hands sought her softness and he filled his arms with her. "But once I did, I couldn't stop."

"I didn't want you to stop. I still don't."

He groaned. "Dammit, sweetheart. What the hell am I going to do about you?"

She lifted upward until her mouth hovered just shy of his ear and she whispered a suggestion that left him shuddering. "How about trying that?"

It took him a moment to shove free an answer. "It's a distinct possibility."

She traced the hard curves of his face. "We'll start again. Touch me the same way you kissed me. No past. No pain. No sorrow. Just a night that's new and fresh and untouched. Is that too much to ask?"

"You want an illusion?" His voice hardened. "You prefer the fairy tale with all the pretense that goes along with it?"

Yes! she almost said. But she realized it wasn't the truth, could never be the truth. How could they appreciate the present without acknowledging all they'd gone through to get there? The past had shaped who and what they were, the good as well as the bad.

"I want whatever you have to give me," she told him. "As long as it's honest."

"Fair enough. If it's honesty you want, it's honesty you'll have. I'm not the person I was and I refuse to pretend I am. But I'll give you what little is left of the man you remember. And—" He hesitated, his throat moving convulsively. "And I'll never lie to you. You...you have my word of honor."

"Oh, Gideon—"

He stared down at her, his gaze more determined than she'd ever seen it. "I haven't said those words since the day the mill burned. But I'm saying them to you, for what it's worth."

She couldn't control the tears then. "Not in all these years? Not even once?"

He shook his head. "There hasn't been any point. I guess I figured you of all people deserve to hear them one last time."

"Not the last," she begged. "Please don't say it's the last time."

His mouth twisted. "Honor's not important to anyone but you, pipsqueak."

"It is important!" she instantly refuted his claim. "To *you*. Haven't you figured that out, yet?"

"You asked for honesty and I'm giving it to you."

He thumbed the tears from her temples with a gentleness he'd have undoubtedly denied. "Sure you don't want the illusion?"

Her lips formed a stubborn line. "We've never pretended with each other and I don't intend to start now." She traced the breadth of his shoulders, reacquainting herself with each familiar ridge and hollow. "Now are you going to take me up on my suggestion, or aren't you?"

She'd provoked an instantaneous reaction. He strained backward, the hallway light cutting a path across features taut with desire. Color rode high on the ridges of his cheekbones and his eyes blazed with a ferocious night-dark glitter. He left the bed and stripped away his clothing with an economy of movement. And then he rejoined her, his hunger impacting like a physical force.

She welcomed him with open arms. It had been so long. Too long. Despite the fact that she'd dated in the past several years, the desire she'd experienced on those occasions had stolen through her veins in bland, distant waves. The temptation to take the moment further had been easy to resist. What she felt now had little to do with such mild, sedate emotions. And the temptation to take the moment as far as possible proved overpowering.

Want stormed through her, ripping her universe into incoherent bits. Only Gideon remained within the center of the chaos, anchoring her in the moment. Once the raging had subsided, they'd talk and she'd tell him the rest. All of it, regardless of what happened as a result. But tonight was for them, the closing of a volume from the past and—she hoped—the start of a new one leading toward the future.

Her fingers dipped into his hair and she tugged him

down to meet her. His mouth was firm and sure, parting to welcome her home. With a soft moan of pleasure, she claimed him as her own. She bit at his lower lip, then soothed it with the tip of her tongue. He reacted to the silent duel with exquisite aggression, initiating a thrust and parry that stoked a white-hot fire, the blaze igniting in the pit of her belly and spreading relentlessly outward.

"Don't stop, Gideon." Stirring beneath him, she fitted herself to him with an instinct undimmed by the years. "Don't ever stop again."

He took her mouth over and over, his kiss becoming one of desperation. "I didn't know," he muttered. "I swear to you, I didn't know it would be the last time."

He sounded so troubled that she hastened to soothe him with an easy smile, a smile that became part of their kiss. "That what would be the last time?"

To her concern, he didn't respond to her reassurance. A darkness settled over him, one she'd have done anything to erase. "The night before the fight, when we made love by the mill. I didn't know it would be the last time we'd be together, the last time I kissed you. I didn't know we wouldn't have a tomorrow. That when I touched you, when I held you, when I heard you whisper my name, when I felt you climax in my arms, that those would be my final moments with you. I didn't know I wouldn't have you close again for five years, or I'd have stamped every second of that night in my memory."

"Oh, Gideon," she murmured, clutching him tighter. "Don't you know I felt the same way?"

He lowered his head, as though bowed beneath an impossible burden. "Afterward... Afterward I tried to remember. I tried to hold on to every moment I could. But it slipped away, faded into echoes.''

"It happens, Gideon. Memories do fade.'' She captured his face once again, forcing him to look at her. "Make love to me and we'll create new ones, ones we'll never forget.''

Her gaze never left his as she slid her hands downward, following the contours of his chest. Tracing the muscular ripples to the flatness of his belly, she reached the source of his desire. He surged against her hand, groaning an encouragement that escaped as half plea and half demand. She didn't need further prompting. She cupped him, stroked his length with slow, indulgent sweeps, reacquainting herself with every scorching inch. He felt incredible, far better than five-year-old memories.

"You're killing me.'' His words escaped through gritted teeth.

She laughed softly. "I'm doing my best. Are you enjoying it?''

"More than you can imagine.'' He pressed her into the pillows, settling into the warm delta between her legs. "Allow me to return the favor.''

He forked his widespread fingers through the tight curls between her thighs until he reached the tip of her scar. Then he backtracked, dipping into her moist heat. Swirling. Stoking. Plying the silken folds until she trembled beneath his hand.

"No more,'' she begged. "I can't bear any more.''

"Sure you can.''

And he proved it by catching the peak of one breast between his teeth, tugging with delicious insistence. At the same time he buried a finger into the very core of her. Every muscle in her body arched in response and a cry caught in her throat. A fluttering began, deep within, and she closed tight around the sweet invasion. She gazed helplessly up at him, silently pleading for the completion that hovered so close. To her profound relief, he didn't hesitate.

"You're mine," he stated, positioning himself between her thighs. "You always have been and you always will be."

"Gideon."

His name finally escaped, the single word an expression of both confirmation and unwavering commitment. He pressed inward, joining them with gratifying speed. She could sense the urgency gathering in him, the overpowering drive to take her, while a conflicting directive forced him to go slow and savor each and every second.

His control was phenomenal. He sheathed himself in her warmth, driving home in a single, powerful stroke. She lifted to meet him, matching the silent cadence with a primal rhythm that sang from the depths of her soul. It must have sung within his, as well, for each of his thrusts matched every one of her parries. They came together again and again, their joining more than a mere mating. Each touch formed a bond, each murmured word a promise, each look a pledge.

Piper clung to him, wishing the moment could last forever. But it slipped away far too soon, the song completed before it had barely begun. Contractions rippled, fisting around him. With a roar, he buried himself to the hilt, spending himself within her. It was all she needed to send her over the edge. Her climax hit hard, the release a painful rapture.

"What have you done to me?" The question burst from her.

He collapsed into her embrace. "I've given you what we've both been after from the moment you came storming back into my life. Whatever you do, don't tell me it was a mistake."

She closed her eyes, unable to move or think, let alone regret. "It wasn't a mistake, I promise. In fact, I'm wondering why we waited this long…and when we can try again."

A noncommittal noise rumbled deep in his chest. "We'll see if you're still feeling so charitable toward tonight's events come morning. I've found the cold light of day often brings a change of heart once the head takes over."

Why would she have a change of heart tomorrow when she hadn't changed it in five impossibly long years? Exhaustion closed around her and she resisted long enough to reassure him. "Come morning my head will be every bit as happy as the rest of me." She even managed a teasing glance. "You have my word of honor."

He cradled her close, snagging the covers and pulling them around her. For a long time he simply watched her. She curled into him, a smile of intense satisfaction curving her mouth. He smoothed her hair away from her face, knowing the time had come for more honesty. He closed his eyes, wishing he'd had the nerve to tell her sooner. "Sweetheart?"

No answer.

"Pipsqueak?"

Her breath came in a soft sigh that spoke of deep sleep and sweet dreams. It didn't matter. Saying it while she slept wouldn't alter the truth any. And hadn't he just promised to always be honest with her? He leaned into her, imprinting the feel of her on his flesh, drinking in the scent of her until he was dizzy with it, tasting the potent nectar of her essence. He branded her in his heart and mind until it burned straight down to his very soul. Something shifted inside of him, offering up a lightness and easing he didn't deserve, but welcomed nonetheless. After being sentenced to what felt like an eternity in pitch darkness, he stepped into reaffirming sunshine.

"I don't know why you still care," he whispered. "I don't know what I've done to deserve such loyalty, considering I'll never be the sort of man you deserve. But I love you, Piper. I always have. And I always will."

A bewildering sense of wrongness woke Gideon. To his amazement, morning had arrived hours earlier. He couldn't remember the last time he'd slept so late. He glanced at Piper, tucked snug within his arms. She hadn't stirred the entire night. It was as though she'd come home and had no intention of moving ever again. He'd had time to sleep on what she'd told him about the fight, and he'd gradually become aware of an elusive "something" that he'd missed during their discussion, a strange insistence growing inside that urged an immediate response.

Gently he eased Piper from his shoulder and onto the pillow. Her breath escaped in a contented murmur and he swept his thumb over the flushed curve of her cheek. Now that he had her back in his life, he'd make certain she stayed there. Once she understood that he wasn't a project requiring a serious overhaul, everything would work out.

Escaping the bed, Gideon padded silently to his study and flipped on the light. His restlessness increased, along with an awareness that he was missing something important. She'd explained about her fall, but a nagging sensation continued to trouble him, a gut instinct he'd learned to trust through painful experience. There was some key bit of information she'd told him on another occasion that held a vital significance—a puzzle piece he needed in order to complete the picture. But he was damned if he could figure out that one final detail.

Piper's boxes were stacked neatly on the floor by his desk and he picked up the first one, opening it. A certainty solidified inside him. Somehow he knew he'd find what he was looking for here, hidden within her photographs.

An hour later, he'd finished sorting through the majority of them. They were all stunning, every last one, revealing an intimate connection with the subjects. He'd long considered it a hallmark of her personal style. But he still hadn't pinpointed what was missing, and it was driving him crazy.

Once again, he scanned the prints he'd spread across his credenza, the ones from her early days. They expressed a raw talent under development and consisted of hundreds of photos of Old Mill Run. Not a single resident had escaped Piper's attention. There were dozens of her family. There were also a handful of the town council. They were all hanging around their favorite gathering spot, the bait and tackle shop, indulging in their favorite activity—a heated discussion over the merits of fishing lures versus live bait. Another showed Mrs. Watz standing in front of her chalkboard expounding on the intricacies of geometric theory and he smiled, remembering how much he'd hated her class—and how much he'd learned from the old bat. And finally there was his mother, tired and drawn, hanging up the laundry while his youngest sister played in a wicker basket at her feet.

What he wanted wasn't there and he scowled. Dammit all! Come hell or high water, he'd get to the bottom of this. She'd told him something significant and he was positive it related to her photographs. Crossing to the coffee table by the couch, he sorted through the pile of her most recent shots. He stirred in discomfort as he studied them. She'd snapped off an entire roll that first day when she'd interrupted his board meeting.

"The not-so-happy people of Happy," he murmured.

There was so much emotion. Anger. Fear. Sorrow. Emotions he'd caused. And then there were the shots taken after Piper had announced that he'd had a change of heart. Joy. Relief. Excitement. Next, he flipped through pictures Piper had taken of his office, and of their contentious drive to Happy when he'd tried to justify buying the Tylers's resort. Last of all, he came across the one of himself stretched out on the couch, the one that showed him at his most vulnerable. Still, he didn't see anything to explain his disquiet.

Returning to his desk, Gideon examined the photos from the years he and Piper had been apart. Most were professional portraits of brides and grooms. To his surprise, there weren't many personal pictures, far fewer than she'd taken during her early years. He paused to peer closely at a couple of photos from right before the fight had broken out, as well as several stark shots of the gutted flour mill. There were also a handful that must have been taken in the months afterward.

Several showed Spencer exhausted and aged beyond his years. And there was even one of Piper. Gideon's brows drew together as he studied it. She sat curled in a protective ball, her face half turned away from the camera, her hair hanging in limp disorder. Had Spencer taken the photo? If so, why? It wasn't a flattering shot. In fact, she looked downright ill.

The phone burred softly beside him and he rested his hip on the edge of the desk. Still staring down at the photo of Piper, he snagged the receiver. "Hart."

"Gideon, thank goodness. Tyler here. I hope I haven't caught you at an inconvenient time?"

"Not at all." His frown deepened as he studied the photograph. "What can I do for you, Bill?"

"Bad news, I'm afraid. The bank's decided to foreclose on our resort. We were given the news first thing this morning."

That captured Gideon's attention. "I'm sorry. I know you were hoping they'd hold off a little longer."

"I…I wondered if you were still interested in doing business."

"I'm still interested in buying you out, yes."

There was a long silence and then Bill spoke again, his voice gruffer than before. "That's all you're prepared to offer?"

Quick and brutal, that had always been Gideon's style. But for some reason he found it more difficult this time around. "I'm afraid so. I don't see any other option."

"All right, fine. I assume you're still willing to pay a fair price?"

"Yes."

"Okay, we accept your offer. And…and thanks."

For some reason, Gideon felt strangely guilty. It didn't make a bit of sense. What the hell did he have to feel guilty about? The man needed help and he was getting it. It might not be in the form Tyler preferred, but that was business, plain and simple. Just like life, it could be harsh and cold and not always pleasant.

"Give me a couple hours to make arrangements at this end and then I'll be in touch," Gideon said.

The minute the conversation ended, Piper opened the door to the study. Coming up behind, she wrapped her arms around his waist and released her breath in a slow, gusty sigh. "Mmm. You feel good."

He turned and folded himself around her, greeting her with a lingering kiss. "Good morning to you, too." Realizing she was dressed, he lifted an eyebrow. "Going somewhere?"

"I'm late enough for work. I'd rather not be any later by lazing in bed the rest of the morning." She smiled at him, her eyes an incandescent blue and filled with the sort of loving expression that eased deep into his soul. "What are you doing?"

Gideon held up the photograph so she could see for herself. "Looking at a picture of you."

He felt her sudden tension. Tiny lines edged her mouth and a bleakness dimmed her gaze. "I didn't realize I'd kept that one."

Interesting. "It's not very good. Who took it? Spence?"

"Yes. About six months after you left town."

She'd confirmed his guess. But what he'd really like to know was... "Why did he take it?"

"As a wake-up call." She shrugged, the irritable movement of her shoulders lacking her usual grace. "He wanted me to see what I'd become."

"Which was?"

"Withdrawn. Emotionally disengaged." She gestured impatiently. "It's all there in the picture."

"Photos don't lie," he repeated.

"As much as I tried to deny it at the time, no. They don't." She stepped farther into the room and glanced around in surprise. "You have my pictures out. Why?"

"I'm looking for something."

She shot him a swift, disconcerted glance, one almost of panic. "In my photos?"

Every internal alarm he possessed went off and his sense of wrongness intensified. "Yes," he confirmed slowly. "I can't get over the feeling that there's something missing. I don't suppose you know what that might be?"

"Not a clue." She plucked the photo from between his fingers and tossed it aside. "Who was on the phone when I first walked in?"

Hell. When she turned the tables, she did it with a vengeance. This was *not* how he'd planned to start his day with her. "Bill Tyler."

She looked up eagerly. "And?"

"And he wanted to let me know that the bank has given him official notice. They plan to start immediate foreclosure proceedings."

Her excitement switched to distress. "Oh, no. Gideon, this is terrible. What are you going to do?"

Quick and brutal, he reminded himself. "Buy his resort." With luck he didn't sound too defensive, though poking out his jaw at a belligerent angle may not have helped his case any.

"Buy the note from the bank, you mean." The optimism in her eyes cut to the bone. "Give him time to turn things around, right?"

Gideon didn't bother to pull his punches. "No."

He'd never realized how painful it would be to witness the death of hope, especially in the gaze of someone he loved more than life itself. She laced her fingers together in a white-knuckle grip. "Gideon, please."

"You're putting yourself in the middle again, Piper," he warned. "It isn't a place you belong."

"Someone has to be there."

"Not you." He picked up the photo she'd discarded, determination taking hold. "If you want to lend me a hand finding what I'm searching for, I'd appreciate the help. But I'm not going to discuss Tyler with you."

She hesitated and he could see how desperately she'd have liked to argue. She must have read his resolve for her expression changed, mirroring the one in the photograph. To his concern an unsettling combination of despair and defeat settled over her. "Are you sure you wouldn't rather let that subject drop, too? Are you positive you want to pursue it?"

"I'm not sure of anything. But gut instinct tells me I'd better figure it out."

"And you always listen to your instinct."

It wasn't a question. "Even when the results might be unpleasant," he confirmed. Her mouth quivered ever so slightly and the truth struck him. How could he have been so blind? She knew. Whatever it was, she knew what he was looking for. He snagged her chin with his index finger and gently tipped her face up to his. "What am I missing, pipsqueak? What's not here?"

He didn't think she'd answer. Then she stepped free of his touch and wrapped her arms around her waist, her breath coming in a long, shuddering sigh. "You were close, Gideon. You followed the progression of the photos. But you've forgotten something. Something from the early days.''

"What?''

She gestured toward the corner of the room. "You're missing some pictures. They're in that box on the floor.''

He glanced at it. It was a small, dusty carton set apart from the others and carefully sealed shut with endless yards of packing tape. He hadn't even realized it held any photographs. It had the look of something that had been closed up tight and shoved into the far corner of a closet where it could remain forgotten. "I thought I had them all. These are the ones I'm missing, aren't they?''

"Let it go, Gideon,'' she whispered.

"What's in the box?''

"You don't want to go there.''

Without a word, he carried it to the desk and sliced it open with a pair of scissors. Slowly he drew out a handful of stills. "Your baby photos,'' he murmured. The missing piece locked into place. "How could I have forgotten them?''

Piper didn't say a word.

"I remember you saying you didn't take baby pictures anymore. For some reason that comment stayed with me. But why are they boxed up like this? It's almost like you're hiding them.'' He frowned, perplexed. "*Why?* Why hide baby—''

She simply stared at him.

It hit him then. He looked at the pictures again and shook his head. If he'd been a praying sort of man, he'd have been down on his knees. "No.'' His voice broke on the word, the sound eerily similar to the cry of a wounded animal. "Please, no.''

CHAPTER NINE

THE photographs tumbled unnoticed from Gideon's hands and he braced himself against his desk, locking his knees in place to keep them from buckling. "You were pregnant when you fell?" He fought for breath, fought to push out words that never should have been uttered—wouldn't have been uttered, if not for him. "You lost the baby? Our baby?"

Tears flooded Piper's eyes, her distress every bit as great as his own. "I'm sorry. I'm so sorry."

His jaw worked for a moment. It took three tries to get the statement out. "I killed our child."

"No!" She was in his arms in an instant, wrapping him up in the sort of loving embrace he didn't deserve. "Spence said the same thing, blamed himself, too. But it was an accident. The mill shouldn't have burned. My brother shouldn't have blamed you. You and he shouldn't have fought. And I shouldn't have interfered. Don't you get it? None of it should have occurred."

He could hear his voice come from far away. "But it did."

"Yes, it did. And no matter how badly we try to change the past, we can't."

"What happened? Just tell me that much."

She opened her mouth, then closed it again. He could feel her start to tremble and he bowed his head until his jaw nestled into the softness of her hair. He wanted to sink into her, lose himself in her. That's all he'd ever wanted. Instead he'd hurt her. The knowledge struck with brutal force. *He'd hurt her.* The one person he'd have protected with his life, he'd left broken on the rocks, their child never to draw breath. And it was all his fault. He shuddered, unable to escape the horrific image.

"Please, Piper. I need to know."

Her arms tightened around his waist and she burrowed into his arms. "After I fell, they took me to the hospital. But all I could think about after the accident was getting to you," she whispered. "No one would tell me where you were or how you were. I should have insisted. I realize that now."

"And I should have found you, regardless of the consequences." A sudden thought occurred to him. "Jasmine swears she gave my note to you. If you were in the hospital—"

"I wasn't. Not the entire time. After they immobilized my shoulder and sewed the cut on my abdomen, I left the hospital against orders." She rested her head on his shoulder, a single tear splashing onto his chest. "Oh, Gideon. It was such a foolish thing to do. I went home to change before tracking you down. That must have been when Jasmine found me. I don't remember getting the note. Or what it said. I must have blacked out right after she left."

Gideon's fingers tangled in her hair and he massaged her nape, absorbing every bit of her pain that he could. "And then?"

"Spencer found me shortly afterward. When I woke up, I was back in the hospital and the baby—" Her breath hitched and it took her a minute to continue. "The baby was gone. I didn't even realize I was pregnant.

Apparently there was a delay with the lab results or they'd have known sooner about my condition. If I'd stayed at the hospital, maybe they could have prevented what happened. Maybe our baby wouldn't have—''

She broke down completely, crying in heartrending silence, as though the pain came from someplace so deep even sound couldn't escape. Tears burned his own eyes and his chest grew tight and full. More than anything he wanted to howl in torment, to give voice to all that Piper had locked away inside. He shook with the need to make it better, to ease both their agony. But there were no words. Even simple speech was beyond him. He didn't say anything for a long time, but simply held her close, trying to give her what strength he had left.

When he felt capable of speaking again, he asked, ''You blamed yourself, didn't you? That's why Spence took the picture?''

She fumbled in her pocket for a tissue and swiped at her wet cheeks. ''You have no idea how many times I've gone over the 'if onlys.' All it does is drive you insane. It happened. There's nothing that can be done. It took me six months to figure out that simple fact. And even then, Spence had to force the issue.''

No wonder he'd been so protective of his sister. And so angry at the man responsible for her anguish. ''If I'd known you'd been injured, I'd never have left you, despite the shotgun and no matter what the sheriff threatened.''

She looked at him, startled. ''You forgot to mention the part about the sheriff. What did he threaten?''

Gideon shrugged. ''He gave me an alternative. I could face charges of arson, attempted murder, resisting arrest and anything else they could think of to throw at me. Or I could leave town.''

"So you left.''

He shook his head. "Don't you believe it. They gave me an hour to pack my stuff and go. Instead I hid out in the woods for two days waiting to hear from you. I didn't give up until Murphy tracked me down and forced the issue.''

"If it makes you feel any better, he's gone now.'' She stroked the bunched muscles of his arm, her touch one of solace. He wanted to protest, explain that he should be comforting her. But somehow he couldn't summon the words. "Not long after the fire, Murphy sold out and left town with his son and daughter.''

"Forget Murphy. Mill Run is better off without his kind.'' He tipped her face up to his. Even such an innocuous caress gave him intense pleasure. "Now I have a question for you.''

"Anything.''

"What would you have done if you hadn't been injured? If you'd gotten my note?''

She didn't hesitate. "I would have asked you to stay and fight. Mill Run was dying. It still is. It needs someone with your drive and determination—the same sort of drive and determination that Spence has—to help fix that. And you needed the family and community that you couldn't find at home. So do your mother and sisters. That hasn't changed, either.''

"You're wrong. I don't need anything or anyone.'' *Except for Piper.* That small truth had become inescapable and he didn't back away from it as he would have days ago. He released his breath in a long sigh. "That's bull, pipsqueak. I need you. I always have and I'm willing to bet I always will.''

The pain eased from her face and she offered up a smile that reminded him of the first hint of dawn breaking through an endless night. Or was it five years of endless nights? "We've always felt the same way, haven't we?''

"About most things.'' He hesitated, facing facts she still wasn't willing to. "But not about everything.''

She made a face. "I know. It would have been difficult to change popular opinion, mainly because Spence was so certain you'd destroyed the mill.'' An urgency threaded her words. "But we could have done it, given time. You still could, Gideon. Together, we can make a difference. Not just in Mill Run. We can help people like Bill Tyler and the jewelers, too.''

He closed his eyes, hating what he was about to do, but knowing that if there were any chance for them, he didn't have any choice. Piper would continue to interfere until he physically moved her out of harm's way. "That's not going to happen.''

"Please, Gideon—''

"It's not going to happen because I'm letting you go.''

Every scrap of color drained from her face. "What are you saying?''

"I know you want to help Tyler. And the jewelry companies. And your brother. But you can't.''

"*You* can,'' she argued.

He shook his head. "I'm going to tear up your brother's note. As of this minute, he doesn't owe me a dime. You don't have any reason to continue staying here. I'll see to it that personnel cuts you a generous check for your services to date.''

''No!'' Her grip tightened around him. ''Don't do this, Gideon.''

''Tomorrow I'll have your things delivered to whatever address you request.''

''Did last night mean nothing to you?''

His control almost broke. ''It meant the world to me,'' he rasped. ''I love you, Piper. I flat-out adore you. And I want you in my life.''

''But?''

''I can't be the person you want.''

''You're already the person I want. You're not hard or cruel,'' she insisted urgently. ''I know you're not.''

''I am when it comes to business.''

''You can't be or you wouldn't forgive Spencer's note.''

She was grasping at straws and they both knew it. ''I'm doing this for you,'' he said. ''I'm doing it so we have a chance.''

''But you won't help the Tylers or any of the others?''

He shook his head. ''Which means you need to think long and hard about the future. You have to accept me as I am, flaws and all. You can't put yourself in the middle every time you disagree with one of my decisions.''

She smiled sadly. ''Don't you get it? That's who I am.'' Her smile wobbled. ''The girl in the middle.''

''And I can't let that continue. I can't have you throwing yourself in the tracks of every oncoming train you see. One of them is bound to run you down. After what you told me about the baby—'' His jaw worked. ''I can't have you hurt again. I want to marry you. I want to rebuild a life together. Have…have children that can know our love instead of being destroyed because of it.''

Her arms fell to her sides. ''In that case, I think we both need to think long and hard about the future.''

''You don't want marriage?''

She shook her head. ''It's not that. *You* may not want to marry *me*.'' She stepped free of his hold and backed away. ''The baby photos, remember?''

He glanced toward the box, his brow creasing in confusion. ''What about them?''

''I didn't stop taking pictures because I lost your baby.'' She paused by the door. ''I stopped because I can't have any more children.''

''What the hell are you doing, Hart?''

Gideon swiveled to glare at Spencer, his breath coming in exhausted gasps. ''I might ask you the same question, considering this is my office and you're here without an invitation.''

''Blame your secretary. She phoned Piper. I intercepted the call and came instead.'' Spence took in the condition of the office with a lifted eyebrow. ''You've been busy. Redecorating, are you?''

''That's none of your damn business,'' Gideon bit out, his tone just shy of a snarl. ''Now that you're here, you can turn around and get the hell out.''

''Sorry. Can't do that. Maybe if you hadn't torn up the note, I'd be willing to go. Or if you hadn't turned Piper into a weepy mess again.''

''Piper?'' That snagged his full attention. ''I've been trying to find her all day. Where is she?''

To his silent fury, Spencer ignored the question. He turned in a full circle, clicking his tongue in admonition.

"You really are in bad shape. This place is a disaster." Strolling farther into the room, he halted by a pile of kindling that decorated the middle of the carpet. "I assume that's your desk. Or what's left of it. I also assume this is why Lindsey called in such a panic."

"My furniture. My ax." Gideon hefted the tool in question, his muscles screaming in protest at the prolonged abuse they'd suffered. He gritted his teeth against the pain and managed to push out a final sentence. "And my choice to use one on the other."

"Can't argue with that logic. Just out of curiosity... What did it do to you? Refuse to deconstruct on demand?"

"Deconstruct?" Gideon's breath escaped in a rush that was part groan and part rough laugh. "You've been talking to Piper."

"She's my sister. Of course I talk to her."

Gideon tossed the ax into the middle of the rubble. It clattered discordantly, gleaming dully amid the ebony remnants. "What are you doing here?" he asked tiredly, massaging his chopping arm.

"Thought I'd have another go at you now that Piper's not around." He stooped beside the remains of the desk. "You really need to do something about your temper, Hart. Why would you want to destroy something this nice?"

"It injured your sister."

Spencer lifted an eyebrow. "Come again?"

"During our...discussion last night," he muttered. "She fell against it and cut herself."

"And because of that you chopped up your desk? A rather drastic response, don't you think?"

Gideon's jaw inched out. "No."

"What about this other stuff?" Spencer gestured toward the rest of the demolished furnishings. "Did all these other pieces attack her? Or was destroying them a preemptive strike in case they went after her, too?"

"Indirectly, yes." Once he'd laid waste to his desk, it had seemed a natural progression to go after the remaining items. Now he wasn't so certain. "At the risk of sounding repetitive, what are you doing here, Montgomery?"

Spencer slowly stood. "I thought we could talk. I mean really talk. Without Piper in the middle."

"Good idea." Gideon inclined his head toward the steps that led to his apartment. "Come on upstairs. As long as you're here, there's something you should see."

Spencer followed him to the study. "First let me say that I appreciate your forgiving the note. I realize it's to move Piper out of harm's way and not because you were overcome by an uncontrollable urge to help me. Even so, I intend to pay back every dime."

"I don't give a damn about the money," Gideon retorted.

"*I* do. If I mention it's a point of honor, maybe you'll understand."

Gideon paused at the door to the study. "Be smart for once in your life, Montgomery. Don't go there."

"Touchy about that issue, are we?"

"You might say that." He crossed to his desk and sifted through Piper's photos. Uncovering the ones he wanted, he tossed them in Spencer's direction. They were a series of shots she'd taken right before the fight had broken out. "I know you don't believe me, so I won't waste my breath repeating this more than once. I didn't burn down your mill."

"So you've said," Spencer replied in an expression-less voice.

Gideon fixed him with an unwavering stare. "I've said it because it's true."

After a long moment, Spencer inclined his head. "Okay. If you didn't do it, then who?"

It was time to put all his cards on the table. Either Spencer believed him or he didn't. At least by presenting his case, he'd have given it his best shot. He couldn't even say why it was so important to convince Piper's brother of his innocence. It simply was. "I have an idea who might have started the fire. But to be honest, we'll probably never know. Not for certain. I wish life were tidy enough to wrap up in a neat little package. But it isn't. It's messy and confusing and full of loose threads."

"You're saying this will always be a loose thread?" Cynicism colored Spencer's tones. "I should simply take your word about the fire, is that it?"

"Personally I don't give a damn whether or not you take my word," Gideon shot back. He gestured toward the photos. "But you might want to look at these. Maybe you'll have the same reaction to them I did."

Spencer joined him by the desk and studied the pic-tures. Residents from Old Mill Run had crowded close to the burning mill, staring at the leaping flames in shock and panic. "These are Piper's," he murmured. "You can't miss her style. I'm not sure she ever showed them to me before."

"They're…unnerving. She might not have wanted to upset you."

"No doubt." Spencer frowned. "Okay, I give. What am I supposed to see?"

"At the start of the fight you claimed someone had witnessed me setting the fire. I thought you were deliberately lying because no one *could* have. Now I'm curious. Who told you it was me?"

"Trish."

"Trish Murphy. Your girlfriend." Gideon tapped a corner of one of the photos. "She's here."

"Of course she's there," Spencer replied impatiently. "She was a witness."

"Look who's standing behind her."

"Her father. Old man Murphy. So?"

"Check out his expression."

Spencer peered closer and swore softly. "I don't believe it!"

"You see it, too, don't you?"

"He's the only one who doesn't seem horrified."

"Horrified? Hell, Spence, he seems damned pleased with himself. I can't help wondering why."

"I can't say for sure. I know he didn't like the Montgomerys any more than he liked your family. You were trash and we were too uppity for our own good. I assumed that changed when I started dating Trish. He didn't seem to mind the idea of his daughter benefiting from a possible marriage." Spencer shook his head. "Who knows why he's looking so pleased. Maybe he enjoyed seeing me taken down a peg or two."

"Especially if I was taken down along with you." He gave Spencer a few more minutes to examine the picture before asking his next question. "Is there any reason you can think of why he'd try to drive a wedge between us?"

"More of a wedge, you mean?" Spencer picked up another photograph. "I see where you're going with this and it doesn't make sense. Do you really think he was twisted enough to burn down my mill to cause trouble between us? Sorry, I can't buy that.''

Gideon shrugged. ''I wouldn't put anything past the man, not considering how much he hated me and my family. But I have to admit, I can't figure what his motivation would be, either. I was hoping you might have some idea. Is there anything? Anything at all?''

Spencer started to reply, then hesitated. ''Trish was always trying to convince me to sell out and leave Mill Run,'' he admitted slowly. ''Her father even took a stab at changing my mind. Said we could pool our money and start over somewhere else. I flat-out refused. My father had been committed to rebuilding Old Mill Run into a booming tourist town and I wanted to ensure his dream became a reality. Not long after I told her there wouldn't be any insurance money, she broke off the relationship. The three of them packed up and left town within the week.''

''Is it possible they thought the mill was insured? Could they have burned it in the hope of forcing your hand? Burn the mill and maybe they'd have a better shot at convincing you to leave Mill Run, money in hand. After all, what would be left to rebuild if the key tourist draw no longer existed?''

''This is what you meant about our never knowing for sure, isn't it?''

''I have to admit, it's sheer supposition on my part and I could be totally off the mark. But the minute I saw these pictures…'' Gideon's laugh had a bite to it. ''What does Piper always say?''

''Photos don't lie.''

Gideon nodded grimly. ''My gut says that what we're seeing here isn't a lie.''

"So's mine." Spencer swallowed. "All this time I thought— I was so certain that you were the one."

"Why? What the hell did I ever do to you?"

"It wasn't what you did."

"It was who I was."

Spencer looked him square in the eye. "I'm not talking about your father or how you grew up. I'm talking about your nature. Piper never saw you the way everyone else did. She only saw the good."

"And you?"

"I saw a dismantler of worlds, never a builder of them. That hasn't changed. At least, not that I can tell." He edged a hip onto the desk. "Piper's told you everything, hasn't she? About the fall and the baby?"

It took Gideon a minute to reply with anything approaching equanimity. "Along with the fact that she can't have any more children. Yes, she's told me."

"And what was your response?" Spencer didn't wait for Gideon to answer. "You took an ax and chopped your desk into kindling."

Gideon's mouth tightened. "Your point?"

"You haven't changed, Hart. And that's a shame. Instead of finding a constructive way of dealing with your pain, you chose the most destructive route available." Straightening, Spencer tossed the photographs onto the desk. "That's why I've worked so hard to keep you two apart. I don't want my sister deconstructed by you. The last time nearly killed her. I won't risk that ever happening again."

Hours later, Gideon returned downstairs and grimly surveyed the ruins of his office. What had Spencer said? That it was in Gideon's nature to dismantle the world around him? Looking at what he'd done to the furnishings, he was forced to admit the truth. It came easily to him. Instinctively. But Spencer had been wrong about one vital fact. Piper hadn't seen only the good in him. She'd seen all of him, the flaws as well as the potential. And still she'd loved him, believed in him.

He realized something else. When she'd put him on that white horse and garbed him in knight's armor, she'd been silently telling him that he could choose to be the hero instead of the villain. It boiled down to choices. He could continue to take, to build an empire on the ruins of the companies he'd dismantled. To deconstruct. Or he could build a future with Piper.

Slowly he stooped beside the remains of the Chippendale cabinet and picked up the stirrup vessel. Miraculously it had escaped damage. Choices, he reminded himself. Was this what he wanted from life? He glanced out the windows and toward the stalwart mountains in the distance.

Or did his future lie along a different path?

He found her by the stream that ran alongside a newly renovated flour mill.

Piper lay in the grass near the water, sound asleep, and Gideon stooped beside her, frowning in concern. Lilac semicircles shadowed her eyes and a tension gripped her, one clearly not eased by whatever dreams she was experiencing. Tenderly he swept a lock of pale hair from her brow, his knuckles brushing the delicate hollow at her temple. She appeared exhausted. Another sin to lay at his feet.

"Pipsqueak?" he murmured. "Wake up, sweetheart."

Her lashes quivered. Stretching, she looked around,

blinking in surprise. "Gideon?" Awareness struck and a dozen different emotions darkened her face. None of them were ones he wanted to see. "What are you doing here?"

"I've come for you, of course." He settled at her side, depositing the present he'd brought in the grass between them. "Did you think you'd escape me this easily?"

She stirred in protest. "I wasn't running away."

"Weren't you?"

"Well, maybe I was. But all things considered, I think it can be excused this once." She pushed herself upright, facing him with typical directness. "If this is about what I told you—"

"That's part of it."

"You're not responsible, okay? It's not your fault. I don't expect anything from you. You can go your way and I'll go mine. Are we clear?"

Ever so gently, he threaded his fingers through her hair. She felt so good. So right. He'd loved her first as a boy, then as a teenager, and finally as a man. But somehow he found himself falling for her all over again. Did she have any idea? If not, he'd make sure he explained it in no uncertain terms. "Oh, we're absolutely clear."

At his touch, she released her breath in a long sigh and leaned into him. He accepted her weight with a small smile, reveling in the feel of her. "Why are you here?" she demanded into his shirtfront. "What's left to be said?"

"There's a lot left to be said. But first I have something to give you." He deposited the gift he'd brought in her lap. "Did I mention? It's a wedding present."

She didn't make a move to touch it. "Funny. I don't recall your asking me to marry you."

He winced. "I'm asking, pipsqueak. Hell, I'm begging." He nudged the box. "Open it. Please."

Reluctantly she picked it up. With slow deliberation, she removed the ribbon, followed by the wrapping paper. After what seemed like an eternity, she opened the flaps and pushed aside the protective packing. "The stirrup vessel?" She appeared less than ecstatic. "Most men go for something more traditional. Like an engagement ring."

"Most men aren't marrying you."

Her jaw tightened. "Let me get this straight. You're giving this to me? You're giving me one of your trophies as a present? And I'm supposed to be pleased? Happy? Or were you hoping to impress me?"

"No. We'll be returning that particular trophy to Archibald Fenzer on our wedding day. Then you're supposed to be pleased, happy—and not to mention—impressed as hell."

She stared at him, stunned. Clearly she hadn't seen that one coming. "Why?" she demanded unevenly. "Why would you do that?"

"Because it's my promise to you," he stated. "A promise that goes even deeper than the promise of an engagement ring."

She stared at him searchingly. For the first time, a spark of hope gleamed in her eyes. "What sort of promise?"

"A promise that I've finally figured out how to climb back on that white horse again. A promise that together we can build a future instead of deconstructing one. A promise that I'll love you to the end of my days." He slipped his other hand into her hair, cupping her head. "We lost our future the day the mill burned. I don't want to lose you, too."

"No, Gideon. We lost one potential future." She lifted her face to his, her breath warm and sweet against his skin. "You'll see. We'll build a new one."

"You can count on it." He couldn't resist any longer. He took her mouth in a slow, passionate kiss and she responded with unstinting generosity. It was a long time before he remembered his other present. "By the way, I have a second wedding gift."

"A ring?"

Aw, hell. He shifted uncomfortably. "No. Not exactly. But that's next on my list. Honest."

She grinned. "It's not another trophy, is it?"

"Nope." He hesitated, struggling to be absolutely honest. "At least... That wasn't what I had in mind when I bought it. I was thinking of making you happy."

Her understanding was instantaneous. "Then it can't be a trophy," she reassured calmly.

"It's the old Miller homestead. I was thinking that after we got married we could move in there and fix it up. I know how crazy you always were about the place." He glanced at her uncertainly. "It'll take a lot of work. But I figured that together we could pull it off."

Tears of joy filled her eyes. "And the resort?" she demanded the instant she recovered enough to speak. "What are you going to do about that?"

"I put Tyler together with the jewelers. Bill's not making it running a ski resort and the others aren't making it in competition with each other. I figured with a little financial backing they could pool their interests. What if we offered a retreat where people could come and mine for their own silver? Meet with local artisans who can design and make handcrafted jewelry from that silver?''

''It's a wonderful idea, Gideon.''

''Bill liked it. So did the others. During the summer they could have conferences for jewelers and designers. Hell, anyone in the business. And in the winter, the Tylers can still run a skiing operation. Happy could become the jewelry capital of the western U.S.'' He shrugged self-consciously. ''It could happen, don't you think?''

''Yes.'' She laughed through her tears. ''It could happen. Miracles happen every day.''

An easing began deep inside, years worth of tension slowly unknotting. ''Sure they do.''

''What changed your mind, Gideon? You were so determined to continue deconstructing.''

He took a long time to answer. ''It was the baby.'' His throat moved convulsively and he wrapped his arms around her, resting his forehead against hers. ''I kept thinking... What if he'd lived? He'd be more than four now. He'd be at an age where he'd start asking questions. And when I looked at my life and what I'd done with it, I wasn't sure I'd want to answer those questions.''

''Why, Gideon?''

His voice grew rough with remembered pain. ''You once told me that no one could take away what I possess because I hadn't built anything worthy of taking. That isn't the legacy I'd planned to pass on to my children.''

At the reminder, a shadow moved across her face. ''I wanted so badly to have your children, Gideon,'' she murmured unsteadily. ''You know that, don't you?''

"Of course I know." His arms tightened around her. "What did the doctors say? Is there any hope?"

She shook her head. "They used words like little to no chance and one in a million and miracle."

"Miracles can happen, Piper."

"You don't understand." She smiled up at him and in that moment he knew nothing mattered as long as he had this woman at his side. "I've already gotten my miracle. You're the only miracle I'll ever need. I love you, Gideon. That's all that's important."

He gathered her close. The sweet odor of the grass beneath them provided a perfume he'd nearly forgotten. At their feet, the creek gurgled a familiar serenade, while the creaking of the mill above them and the gentle chirping of the crickets made him realize something vital. He'd missed this. Missed it more than he'd have ever suspected. At some point, when he hadn't been paying attention or been too self-absorbed to care, the essence of Old Mill Run had crept deep into his bones. It had lodged there, quiet and enduring, remaining even during the years he'd been absent. No matter how hard he'd tried to deny it, the town and his experiences within its boundaries had forged the man he'd become. And he realized something even more vital.

He'd returned home and he didn't intend to leave ever again.

"I love you, too, pipsqueak," he whispered. "And I swear, I'll do everything in my power to make you happy. You have my word of honor."

Piper closed her eyes, her happiness complete. His last few words had slipped out with breathtaking ease, as unconscious as they were heartfelt. Whether he knew it or not, they were the ultimate proof that she had, indeed, received her miracle. It had been a long, rough road. But now that they had made it back home, she truly didn't need anything else.

EPILOGUE

During the years that followed....

TWILIGHT had settled over Colorado, blanketing the foothills in peaceful shades of rose and lavender. Golden light flickered to life throughout the thriving community of Old Mill Run, spearing outward toward the more remote homes found on the outskirts of town. It spread across Spencer's Mill, now in operation and a huge tourist draw, and across Hart Construction, which had at one time been a run-down trailer park.

The name was something of a misnomer because it wasn't an operation that constructed buildings, but was owned by a man who had an uncanny knack for turning the most disastrous companies into successful operations. Businessmen from all over the country came here for advice, and occasionally a helping hand, both of which were provided with unstinting generosity.

A few miles out of town, one house in particular glowed with life, tucked close into the embrace of the Rocky Mountains. It was the old Miller place, a huge homestead that had been left to suffer into ruin. But loving hands had changed all that, renovating it over the ten years since its purchase.

The exterior reflected the most obvious changes. Gardens profuse with flowers wreathed the house and fresh paint gleamed on the clapboard siding and surrounding buildings. Prosaically a porch swing stirred gently in the breeze, creaking a welcome to approaching visitors. And the stained-glass front door showed a boy and girl sitting side by side fishing in a stream that ran alongside of an old mill.

The interior had seen as dramatic a change as the exterior. A photographic studio occupied what was once a dusty attic. Black-and-white photos abounded, including many that had won national awards. And though it was off-limits except to a select few, the dictate was an unusual exception in an otherwise warm and accommodating home.

A huge, modern kitchen had become a natural gathering place for friends and relatives, and what was laughingly referred to as the formal dining room was anything but. Nor did the spacious living room offer any such decorum. The only suggestion of formality came from the framed photos that lined the walls. But even that small pretense was negated by the poses.

The first was of a naked baby standing in an old metal washtub. A black-eyed glare warned of a pugnacious nature, as did the cheeks flushed with temper. Most telling of all, a bright red washcloth winged a path toward the photographer. The second picture was of a young girl—no more than four—dressed in her mother's wedding clothes. She stood on wobbly heels, a string of pearls encircling her neck and hanging to her knees. Her pale blond hair fell ruler-edge straight from beneath a cockeyed veil that nearly obscured her face. But it couldn't obscure the sweetness of her smile or the enormous light blue eyes that peeked out from beneath the mounds of ivory lace and tulle.

Next came a photo of a young boy, his wayward dark hair ruffled by a breeze as he hammered home the finishing nail into an impressive tree fort. The camera had caught that final moment of accomplishment—the boyish chin set at a determined angle that hinted at the compelling man he'd someday become, his blue-gray eyes awash with jubilation, his grin one of ultimate triumph.

And last of all was a photo of a girl, clearly the oldest of the four. She was dressed in jeans held together by holes and sheer determination. Her shirt was missing more buttons than remained, and it had been haphazardly shoved into her jeans. Her light hair hung in uneven braids to her waist and her black gaze warned of a ferocious energy. Around her neck hung her very first camera and she crouched beneath a tree, preparing to take a photo of a fledgling screech owl's inaugural flight.

The first impression most visitors received when they saw the photos was the skill with which they'd been taken. Their next comment came the second they noticed that the pictures were no longer completely black-and-white—a departure for this particular photographer. The faintest hint of color had invaded the shots, adding depth and light and joy to each. Some preferred the old style. Others relished the new. But to a person, they agreed on one vital fact.

These were photographs of miracles. And the four "miracles," as they were affectionately called, were raised by parents who adored them, in a town that became known to tourists far and wide as a modern-day Brigadoon. It was a timeless place, built into prosperity by the Hart and Montgomery families, a place where love abounded and happiness was guaranteed. For through their love for each other Piper and Gideon discovered one simple truth.

Miracles do happen.

Modern Romance™
...seduction and
passion guaranteed

Tender Romance™
...love affairs that
last a lifetime

Sensual Romance™
...sassy, sexy and
seductive

Blaze
...sultry days and
steamy nights

Medical Romance™
...medical drama on
the pulse

Historical Romance™
...rich, vivid and
passionate

MILLS & BOON®

Winner at

2001 **IDEA** INTERNATIONAL
DESIGN
EFFECTIVENESS
AWARDS

MAT5

Coming in July

❧

The Ultimate Betty Neels Collection

❧

✳ A stunning 12 book collection beautifully packaged for you to collect each month from bestselling author Betty Neels.

✳ Loved by millions of women around the world, this collection of heartwarming stories will be a joy to treasure forever.

2 FREE

books and a surprise gift!

We would like to take this opportunity to thank you for reading this Mills & Boon® book by offering you the chance to take TWO more specially selected titles from the Tender Romance™ series absolutely FREE! We're also making this offer to introduce you to the benefits of the Reader Service™—

- ★ FREE home delivery
- ★ FREE gifts and competitions
- ★ FREE monthly Newsletter
- ★ Exclusive Reader Service discount
- ★ Books available before they're in the shops

Accepting these FREE books and gift places you under no obligation to buy, you may cancel at any time, even after receiving your free shipment. Simply complete your details below and return the entire page to the address below. *You don't even need a stamp!*

YES! Please send me 2 free Tender Romance books and a surprise gift. I understand that unless you hear from me, I will receive 4 superb new titles every month for just £2.55 each, postage and packing free. I am under no obligation to purchase any books and may cancel my subscription at any time. The free books and gift will be mine to keep in any case.

N2ZEA

Ms/Mrs/Miss/Mr ....Initials......................................
BLOCK CAPITALS PLEASE

Surname ....

Address ....

....

....Postcode................................

Send this whole page to:
UK: FREEPOST CN81, Croydon, CR9 3WZ
EIRE: PO Box 4546, Kilcock, County Kildare (stamp required)

Offer valid in UK and Eire only and not available to current Reader Service subscribers to this series. We reserve the right to refuse an application and applicants must be aged 18 years or over. Only one application per household. Terms and prices subject to change without notice. Offer expires 31st July 2002. As a result of this application, you may receive offers from other carefully selected companies. If you would prefer not to share in this opportunity please write to The Data Manager at the address above.

Mills & Boon® is a registered trademark owned by Harlequin Mills & Boon Limited.
Tender Romance™ is being used as a trademark.